Infidelity

Infidelity

RAHSAAN AKI TAYLOR

J. Kenkade
PUBLISHING®

LITTLE ROCK, ARKANSAS

Infidelity
Copyright © 2019 by Rahsaan Taylor

J. Kenkade Publishing
6104 Forbing Rd
Little Rock, AR 72209
www.jkenkadepublishing.com
Facebook.com/jkenkadepublishing

J. Kenkade Publishing is a registered trademark.

Printed in the United States of America
ISBN 978-1-944486-62-4

This book is dedicated to a true rider, my provider and soldier– my big sister with the big heart, Shekila Moore-Jones. I love you more than words can express, so I dedicated a book to you. Keep your head up, stay strong, and keep the faith. It gets greater later. You sacrifice so much so your kids can have the finer things in life. You are a wonderful mother, woman, sister, and child of God!

-Your "lil' bro, Rahsaan Taylor

"When a person shows you who they are, believe them!"

-Maya Angelou

Chapter 1

Ooooh! Chad grabbed the bottle of lotion from off the desk and squirted another massive round into his hand. He peered at the visual on the screen and began to stroke his limp penis. He flipped through the pictures on the monitor until he found his most desirable pose. It took him a while to locate the exact photo because he had about 1,426 inappropriate pictures that he enjoyed.

"Wow! This feels so good." He moaned, as he continued to jerk on his full erection.

It didn't take him long to skeet his juices into the Charmin toilet tissue.

He sighed, bobbing his neck back and forth before he finally decided to lean his back against the chair. He was in ecstasy – lightheaded but feeling exhilarating. He sat there, admiring his collection for the next minute or so before he realized that he needed to clean himself off.

Chad flopped backwards, and the wheels on the chair automatically complied. He swiveled around, gapped one of his heavy leg, got the side, then rose up. His knees buckled because they were weak from the encounter earlier, but he managed to sustain his balance. He whistled all the way down the hall to the bathroom. Next, he removed the soap from the soap dish and began to wash his monkey-looking paws. He looked down at his pantleg and saw that the excess semen had skeeted on them. So, he grabbed a wad of tissue paper and wiped the spot clean.

After he was finished, he looked in the mirror, rubbed both of his cheeks, and said "You handsome fellow, you. How do you do the magnificent things that you do?"

He smiled, then walked out of the bathroom. He headed back towards his favorite spot in the whole wide world – his seat at the computer. He pressed the keys on the pad to enter his most expedient website, and a live chat room came up when he clicked the mouse.

"Whoa."

He jerked his head back because he was excited to see someone already present on the webcam.

"Hi. How are you doing?" He asked, after he fixed his webcam to focus completely on him. "My name is Chad. What is your name?"

"My name is Lily," the girl answered back.

She was looking out of place or as if she were forced to be there.

"Is there anyone with you?"

"Yes, my mommy is right there." She pointed to the left of her.

From out of nowhere, a woman popped up on the screen. Unlike her daughter, she had on more than just a bra and panties. She was actually well-groomed. Her height wasn't average. She favored an Amazon woman.

Chad's face dropped. He'd never been caught in the

chat room in a particular scenario like this one before. He didn't know what to say. For a minute, he figured that he was about to be put on blast. He was afraid of jail, but, somewhere in his mind, he had made himself believe that what he was doing was appropriate. Plus, they were only speaking on the computer.

"Don't fret, young man. I'm just here to offer my daughter up to you in the most useful way." The woman finally spoke up.

"And what way may that be?"

The Amazon looked at him with a rigorous stare on her face.

"I'm not here to play a game with you."

She copped a nasty attitude with him.

"What other type of 'useful way' do you think that I'm talking about? There's only one way that I know of."

She walked up to the screen and stretched her arm forward as if she was about to cut the monitor off.

"Business has always been business to me. It's 'get in, get the money, let the customer get what he or she wants, then get out'. It's that simple, but if you want to play like you're slow, thank you, I'll just alert another potential buyer."

"Hold up!"

Chad gestured with his hand, signaling for them to freeze.

"You just wait a minute now. I've been procrastinating because I've never been in a live chat room with an actual adult before. But I am willing to take up the offer on your daughter."

He peered back over at the little girl.

"And she's a hot commodity, too."

"Okay, then first we have to get a substantial agreement."

"And what may that be?"

"I'll transport her to you, and you can have physical intercourse with her for three hundred and fifty dollars. Or you can have cybersex with her for one hundred and seventy-five dollars."

Chad was baffled. He'd never actually had sexual contact with any type of female before; all he had known his whole life were penthouse magazines, Playgirls, and sexual images from his valuable computer. Over the years, he had transitioned from looking at photos of full-grown women to adolescents. It was something strange that clicked in his mind and preferences that made him no longer get aroused by adults.

"Uh. Let's see...I'm willing to take the physical intercourse for three hundred and fifty dollars," he said excitedly, while rubbing his hands. His mouth was watery because he was finally about to touch a live girl in ways that he had only imagined after his twenty-two years of living.

"Are you aware that she's underage and being purchased on the market?"

"Yes, I know that! That's exactly why I came to this particular website. I get off on young girls."

"Okay, that's our cue."

The lead agent took off his earpiece because he had recorded enough.

"Let's move!" he told the guy in the driver's seat.

They were posted three trailers down from Chad's residence. Slowly, the unmarked van rolled until it pulled up in front of lot number nine. Once the driver parked the vehicle, seven agents jumped from out of the back door.

"You, guard the back entrance. You, cover the left side windows, and you, cover the right side."

He directed his team proficiently, as he always did.

"Miranda, you come with me."

While the other agents diligently followed their orders, Captain Smith and Lieutenant Thompson moved towards the front entrance. Every deputy was well-trained for these specific events. On their way to the assigned location, they scrutinized their surroundings and peered through every window in the house.

"Cobra Four, this is Eagle Blue."

One of the agents decided that it was time to report.

"I have the suspect on deadlock," he whispered into his walkie talkie. "He is at the East wing of the residence. It seems as if the Charlatons still have him occupied."

"Good job, Eagle Blue. Keep a visual on him. I'm about to knock at the door to gain his attention."

"10-4."

Static emitted through the transmitter.

Chad was still setting up an appointment inside his house. He couldn't wait until his discussion with the girls was over. Then, he could finally get down to the real business. His mouth was super watery, and his little pecker stood at full attention. Just when he was about to wrap up their conversation, he heard a strange knock at the door.

"Shoot!" he exclaimed to himself.

"Excuse me," the woman said with a serious look on her face. "What was that?"

"Aw, it wasn't anything important...just a knock at the door. So, if you would pardon me, then I'll be back quicker than you can say Peter Pecker picked a pack of peppers."

"All right, then."

The two females looked at each other and winked.

When Chad got out of the chair, he almost fell to the floor. He was fuming that someone had interrupted his most pleasant moment. Once he made it to the front door, he glanced through the peephole but didn't see anyone.

"I bet that's them got-dang kids playing at my door again."

He balled up and folded his fist, then began to walk off speedily. By the time he made it halfway into the hallway, he heard another knock at the door. '

"Who is it?" he yelled to the top of his lungs.

"The FBI. We have a warrant for your arrest. So, open up, or we'll be force to enter by our own will."

"What?!"

Chad instantly became paranoid. He ran to the window and saw the unmarked van parked outside. He glanced again through the peephole and saw deputies standing in the center of his porch.

"If you truly are feds, then let me see your identification."

The captain reached inside his vest, then pulled out the proper I.D. badge and revealed it to Chad.

"Mr. Rosenbeck, you are going to be detained for child pornography and attempted statutory rape. Don't try to elude us because we have your house completely surrounded."

Chad was nervous. He couldn't stop biting on his fingernails.

"All right. I'm about to open the door. But first let me put on some clothes."

He ran down the hallway in panic mode. He kept turning around in circles as if he were lost in his own home. The first thing that popped into his head was to talk to the females who were waiting for him on his computer screen. Without a shadow, he moved his overweight body into the master bedroom.

"Excuse me, ladies, but I have a sudden situation on my hands that needs immediate attention. I don't know why, but the FBI is at my front door!"

"We know."

"What?"

"I said we know," the amazon replied, while sucking her teeth.

"Yeah, we know the FBI is at your door because we are the ones who sent them there," Lily asserted. "We've been tracking you for a long time. You are a very sick man, Mr. Rosenbeck. The Bureau knows that you have over a thousand inappropriate photos on your CPU. And with the conversation that you engaged in with us today, we are sure that you will be gone from the streets for a very long time."

"Who are you?"

"My name is Lily Stevenson, and I am an FBI agent."

Both of the ladies flashed their badges to him against the video screen.

"This is entrapment. You tricked me into thinking you were a minor," he cried. "You can't make me believe that this will substantially hold up in court."

"It can...and it will."

He was devastated. No one and nothing had ever outsmarted him before. He always figured that he was the cleverest one.

"I can't go to jail. I refuse to do it. Ain't no telling what them guys are going to do to me in there."

"Attention, Cobra Four!"

"Go ahead, Eagle Blue."

"I still have a visual on the perpetrator. The subject is suspiciously rummaging around in his closet. His gestures and behavior seem to be very belligerent."

"Keep contact on him. And tell me what he grabs out of the closet."

"Okay, he is turning around now. He has what appears to be a twelve-gauge shotgun. Would you like for me to take him out?"

"Negative! Do not take a shot at him yet. But everyone remain on standby. I don't want any blood to be shed that doesn't have to be. But if he can't be subdued, then everyone has my permission to take him all the way out!"

"Copy that."

Chad grabbed his limited-edition Winchester and loaded it up with slugs. He walked toward the front door and thought about holding court in the middle of the streets, but he reconsidered. He figured that just because he was a wuss, he couldn't take an innocent person's life. Besides, the rangers were just there to do their job. Hesitantly, he paced back and forth in the middle of the hallway. He didn't know it, but he was positioned in a blind spot to the federal agents.

They waited for him to make his next move. All the agents stood still. They scrutinized every aspect of the situation. Everyone knew that not being ready for the least expected could have a deadly outcome. The captain and cadets stood firm, with their guns pointed to blast. They were blinded because they lost visual on what was now a potential threat.

Back inside the trailer, Chad was now sitting on the floor with his back against the wall. He was covered with sweat, and his breathing capacity had slowed all the way down. Within an instant, he had cocked the pump and shoved the barrel down the back of his throat. With regretful tears in his eyes, he squeezed the trigger.

"Come on. Let's go, let's go! Move."

The captain rushed with the order after he heard the first gunshot.

The investigators didn't hesitate to kick in the door. They cautiously maneuvered through the home. Checking in every hidden spot, they motioned with special attention until they stumbled upon the body of Chaderick Rosen-beck. The young sergeant couldn't stand the stench. He got dizzy from the sight of the blood and brain fragments. He ran to the side and vomited.

"Is this his first body?"

Captain Smith Lieutenant Thompson didn't speak. She nodded her head indicating yes.

Chapter 2

Todd and Mark were behind the cash registers at Auto Zone. They were watching as two women entered the building, wearing tight shorts that exposed their toned legs.

"Hi, boys," one of the ladies said in a seductive way. She waved then watched as the guys rubbernecked over the counter until she was out of their view.

"Man, I love summertime," Mark screamed while convulsing. "I love those sisters. There's just something about that dark chocolate I like."

"Whatever, man."

Mark looked at Todd inconspicuously then went to stacking the shelf that was behind him.

"Do you want to know what I heard?"

"What's that?" he answered without turning around.

"I heard that white girls' honeypots are cold, and black girls' is hot."

He put his finger on the side of his head and thought about what he had just said before he decided to rephrase his statement. "Well, white girls' insides are not cold like an icebox, but theirs are cooler compared to black girls. Basically—" he said excitingly. "—I heard that black twat is really hot!"

"And how do you know this?"

"I don't exactly know how it feels, but I know it tastes kind of like water–Aquafina, to be exact. And it's really... really wet."

Mark looked incredulous.

"Don't tell me that you let a female beat you for your head!"

"What do you mean she beat me for my head?"

"She got one over on you, man!" he said obnoxiously.

"Nah. It wasn't anything like that. We were both smoking weed one day, then she got to acting extremely freaky. She sat in my lap and began to rub her finger across my jaw. After that, we started kissing."

"Uh-huh."

"Next, she asked me to eat her out."

"And?" Mark sneered sarcastically.

"So, I did it, and she came like two or three times. I started pulling my pants down, and, out of the blue, she told me that she wasn't feeling well, so it'd be best if I hurried up and left because her friends were on the way to her house."

"And you believed her?"

"Yeah, I figured she was trying to look out for me. She said that she didn't want to see a white guy get caught by himself in the Southside Projects. You know, those projects is really rough over there," he added with a little more emphasis.

"That is exactly what I was talking about."

Mark laughed harder than he ever had before.

"Man, you are totally a dufus."

"What are you insinuating?"

"Like I've already said, you got beat out of some head. Sit down and listen. Let me put you up on game."

He didn't finish his lecture until Todd followed his instructions to sit on the counter.

"It's like when a man deceives a girl into giving him a blowjob then leaves her in the motel room. It's like when a guy gets him some coochie from a girl, kicks her outta his car, and never calls her again. Just to narrow this thesis down…you got played, but it's sad because you don't even know it."

"I have arrived, boys!" a delicate voice sang out, interrupting their conversation.

"You're late," Todd and Mark simultaneously scolded while vigorously pointing their fingers.

"As usual," one of the guys said playfully.

"I don't know why, but my raggedy alarm clock just didn't seem to buzz this morning," Ann said, while rushing to put her purse underneath the counter. She adjusted her clothes then continued her statement. "I have to get somebody to look at that damn thing."

"Do you try actually setting the alarm clock on it?" Todd inquired.

"Well, yeah," she replied giddily. "Of course I did. It stays set on the same time that I've always had it. Duh!"

"Next time, slide the little switch over on the top of the clock that says 'on.'"

Mark gestured. "It's the button on the clock that turns the alarm on."

"Yeah, because the alarm clock dilemma is getting old."

"I have used that excuse about four or five times already,

haven't I?"

She glared at the men, but they didn't respond.

"I'll put on my things-to-do list to make sure that I come up with another excuse for being late next week."

"Make sure it's reasonable."

"Don't worry, I will. You see how many times y'all went for that alarm clock thingy without complaints?"

"So, that's what you do? You sit at home and think of a way to get one over on us?"

"Trust me, honey, it doesn't take that long to think of a scheme for you two."

Todd's mouth dropped.

"Girl, you are really something serious."

They all laughed together before they were interrupted by the two ladies who entered the store earlier.

"Excuse me, but can we get some service up in here if y'all ain't too busy joking and laughing?" one of the customers asked.

"Aw. Forgive us. We was just entertainin' ourselves to pass time," Todd replied. "You should know how that goes."

He looked at the ladies to respond, but they didn't. "You do have a job, don't you?"

"Boy! Don't be asking us no questions. Trying to get all up in our personal business.

Just do your job before you don't have one."

Todd obediently grabbed the anti-freeze and bottle of windshield wiper fluid from the older girl. He scanned the barcode and rang up their total. Mark and Ann were marveling in the background. They didn't know whether to burst out and laugh in Todd's face at that moment or wait until later on. However it went down, they were going to let him know that he got checked by a female, so he would need to man up from then on.

"Your total comes out to eleven dollars and thirty-four cents."

"Here you go." She pulled out a wad of cash and gave him a fresh bill with Andrew Jackson on the front of it.

"I hope that I'm not intruding, but I have to compliment you ladies on how beautiful you are."

"Mmm-hmm," she murmured without taking her eyes off the exchange of her money. She counted her return then began to walk off but was called back by the cashier.

"I was wondering if it would be all right for me to take you out to eat or something?"

"I'm not hungry."

"Then just maybe…" he stuttered. "We could get something to drink."

"I'm not thirsty." She tried to walk off again.

"Look!" He sounded desperate. "You are a gorgeous woman. As a matter of fact, you're one of the finest queens that I've ever seen. And I just can't go on without making an advance toward you. My grandpa always told me to never let anything that's worth it get away from me."

"Well, thanks, but no thanks for the advancement. And besides…I'm spoken for. I'm married." She speedily showed the ring on her finger before her friend had the chance to answer any questions.

"You lying," Todd declared angrily. "That's the wrong finger you showed me. The married finger is the index finger. You basically just flipped me off. Are you trying to tell me something?"

The two women gazed at each other and giggled before

they stormed out of the store.

"Man, I'm going to be the first one to say it. You have absolutely no game!"

Mark came up and placed his hand on Todd's shoulder.

"What was up with that line about your grandpa always telling you to never let anything that you like get away from you?" He asked in a humorous tone. "You are so lame."

"How are you gonna try to talk to one of the girls at first than end up trying to get with the other one?" Ann wanted to know. "Please explain that to me."

"The first one was letting me know that I was playing on the wrong court, so I had to shoot my jumper the other way."

"What type of metaphor is that?"

"It's a man's contingent. You wouldn't understand."

"Help me understand." She smirked, while getting louder. "Please enlighten me on this logic."

"Being a man, the first rule is to never let any woman inside the sect," Todd said. "That'd be like letting my left hand know what my right hand is doing."

"You know what?" Ann raised her hand for him to stop talking. "I'm not about to let you worry me with your sinner ordeal. I'm going to let Mark handle you."

"What you mean by Mark gonna handle me? Mark ain't got no game."

"I got more game than you."

"Do you really think so?"

"Yeah. I know I so."

"Then we are going to see. The next woman who comes in this door – you have to get her phone number before she leaves."

"All right. That's a bet."

"What's the bet?"

"One days' work."

"Okay."

As they were speaking, the bell on the entrance door sounded off. A young lady with her hyper son walked in.

"Come on, boy. I'm not playing with you." She dragged him in, but he barely budged.

"Well, here's your chance to prove Todd wrong," Ann whispered to Mark.

"Excuse me," Mark announced his presence boldly. "But is there any way that I can be of any assistance to you?"

"Not really," the customer said politely. "I'm only here to pick up a few items then leave…" She glanced down at her child. "If I can get this knuckleheaded boy to cooperate."

"What's the problem, man? You seem to be having a difficult time keeping up with your mother."

The child didn't respond. He folded his arms together and looked at Mark grossly.

"Aw. He'll be all right." She grabbed her son's hand then led him down the aisle. "He's upset because he couldn't go over to his favorite cousin's house."

"But you told me I could go," he proclaimed stubbornly after he stopped walking.

"That was before my car started running hot."

"That's dangerous, lil' man, for a car to run hot. It could blow up or catch on fire. Then you can't ever go to your cousin's house again."

They looked at him as if he were making a lot of sense.

"Now do you want to miss going over to your cousin's house just one time then when your mom's car can get fixed, you can go and have all the fun you want? Or do you want the car to burn up so you can't ever have a ride to go over there again?"

"She could have dropped me off before the car got fixed."

"Your cousin's house wasn't in this direction that she had to come to get the car fixed." The six-year-old pointed toward the East wing of the building.

"It's right down the street."

The boy's mother started at Mark like her eyes were saying "He got you now, so what have you got to say about that one?"

"What is your name, lil' man?"

"Marcus. What's your name?"

He had an incredulous glare on his face after the child's answer.

"Take a guess what my name is."

"Your name's probably something lame like Bob, Pete or Steven. Am I right?"

"You are completely wrong. My name is something cool like Mark."

"Wow! That's like my name," he pronounced excitedly.

"So, we have something in common now."

"That is correct."

"Say, Marcus. Why don't I take you down this other aisle to show you this brand new remote control vehicle that we just got in? And, while we do that, your mom can go shop in peace."

He motioned to the mother to get her approval. "Is that all right with you?"

She thought about it momentarily.

"Sure, go ahead." She waved them off dismissively with a

bright smile on her face.

Within seven or eight minutes, Marcus came from around the corner, whipping a yellow hummer with the remote controller.

His mother was already checking out at the cash register, so he gently bumped the front of the SUV into her.

"Boy!" She jumped while simultaneously looking down. "You better watch where you going."

"I'm sorry, Momma." He snickered with a sinister grin.

"Go put that truck back up and come on so we can go home."

"This is my truck now."

"No, it's not. I can't afford that truck, so go put it up before you break it."

"Aw. Don't worry about it, Mrs.—?" Mark walked toward her with his hand stretched out.

She shook his hand and said, "Sherie."

"A gift from me to him. So, don't worry about the vehicle and batteries. It'll be put on my account."

Sherie marveled. No one ever made such a brazen move for her child like that before. She was pleased but rather suggestive. "Thanks," she replied.

"It's nothing. A small thing to a giant like myself. Even though I don't have any kids, I know the responsibilities and joy of parenting. But more importantly, I know how much a woman needs a break."

"That's interesting."

"I mean, think about it. Men have all the breaks that they want. They go over to their boys' houses, clubs, or games without ever involving the mother of their child. That's why every chance that I get, I try to give a woman space, so she can regain peace of mind during the day."

"A'ight now, Mark. You gonna make me say that you can take him home with you," she said jokingly.

"Actually, I would appreciate that. I mean, I would like to grow a bond with little man. So if it's all right with you and the father, I would like to take Marcus to the movies, a game, or the river park sometime."

"Whoa! Can I go, Momma?" Marcus clutched her leg and begged. "Please!"

"His father is not involved in his life."

"I'm sorry to hear that." He put his head down and buckled his lips like he was sad. But, in reality, he was happy on the inside to hear that a man wasn't in their lives.

"And I don't know you like that. People don't let a complete stranger run off with their child."

"You can trust me." He crossed his heart. "I promise loyalty with scout's honor."

She giggled. "You is kinda cute and convincing. So, I'll tell you what…you can take us." She pointed towards herself then toward Marcus. "To the movies or a sports event."

"Okay, fine," he said pleasantly. "How does Friday around seven sound?"

"Good. Where's a pen so I can give you my number?"

Mark instantly looked at Todd, who in return was staring at the new acquaintances from behind the cash register. He speedily found an ink pen.

Sherie wrote down the number, handed it to Mark, and exclaimed. "Sevenish. Tomorrow night."

Marked nodded his head, indicating a yes.

She walked out of the store, swinging her voluptuous hips from side to side.

"So, you decided to go for the soft spot and prey on the woman with the child, huh?" Ann asked.

"That's just how you have to do it sometimes. Conversation may rule the nation, but soft spot is a penetrating vibration."

"Sweet."

There was a moment of silence before Mark broke the ice. "Oh, yeah. Todd, I know that tomorrow is your off day, but, due to our bet, you'll be coming in to work with Ann and Shane. Because I have some business to attend to."

Todd never responded. He stood there obediently with a dumbfounded expression on his face.

Chapter 3

The young detective made his way through the crowd. "Excuse me. Whoa! I'm sorry. Pardon me. My apologies." He occasionally bumped into several individuals because he was struggling to keep the many folders attached under his arm.

"Ay, yo. Agent Ross," a man yelled from a distant corner in the facility. "I've been wondering what goes on in the rape division. Your last investigation ended with a suicide scene, so a real man had to come out to do your job for you. As a matter of fact, when was the last time that you guys apprehended any of your suspects? There are so many who got away, I'm starting to think that you are working with them perverts. Besides…you look like one yourself."

He raised up both of his arms. "Now, you do know that I am internal affairs, right? So, don't make me have to put some heat on you guys to force you to do your job accurately."

Agent Ross was embarrassed to be put on the spot like that. He raised his cup of coffee into the air, as everyone looked and laughed at him. "What makes all of your jobs more important than ours?"

"We have vast responsibilities, and we actually catch hideous criminals, for instance. Donnie, what type of work are you into?"

"I'm in the homicide division."

"Joseph, what type of duties do you endure?" The internal affairs deputy asked.

"I'm with the bomb squad," Joseph responded, with a smirk on his face.

"Hold up. Wait a minute."

He stopped Agent Ross in his tracks before he could fade away. The internal affairs deputy wanted to taunt him some more.

"Now, here's a woman with a more dangerous and sophisticated job than yours. Sharonda, will you please enlighten us with your tasks?"

"I'm with the drug task force," she exclaimed from across the room. "We go after ruthless kingpins, cartels, organized crimes, and conglomerates that are prominent."

"Well, that's just great. I see that you guys really love your jobs. I hope you have wonderful and long careers, but I have to scramble because I'm late for briefing."

They all mocked him as he ran away.

By the time Sergeant Ross made it into the room, his team had already started the meeting without him.

"It's nice for you to finally join us," the captain announced arrogantly. "I know that you are new to this team—" He looked at his watch. "—but you are five minutes late, and tardiness will not be tolerated. But go ahead and grab a seat. Luckily, you haven't miss much, so we'll be able to bring you up to speed.

"Yes, sir!" He stood upright, saluted, then took a seat

next to his colleagues.

"Now, our mission as crime stoppers is to subdue these insane individuals. Believe it or not, most of them don't have a conscience." Captain Smith pressed a button on the remote control, and the images on the projection screen automatically flipped. "Thus far, we have had a staggering year."

"Yeah, I remember him well," Lieutenant Thompson assured the group once she saw the photo of a guy who she arrested by herself.

"Of course you do. We all remember him," another one of the officers asserted. "That's the same guy who put that nasty mark on your face."

That last statement caused an uproar in the room. Everyone had their own opinion about the matter. There was so much commotion from everyone trying to speak at the same time that eventually no one could be clearly understood.

"Okay, guys!" Captain Smith yelled loudly. "Let's stay on track here. Our aim is to focus on these criminals who pollute our society and affect people's minds, bodies and souls. Right now, as we speak, someone is scheming about their next attack. Some victim is about to get hurt. And someone, somewhere, somehow is about to commit an atrocious sin. Our job is to be there before it happens. If we can't prevent it, at least we can solve the case after it happens, so we can give these innocent people some type of closure."

"You are right. That is what we are here for!"

"I have a question." Officer Ross raised his hand. "Let's say that we are put in a situation like the one that occurred the other day. You know, like with the dead man and all."

"When you threw up all over your clothes," one of the officers said jokingly to another, not knowing that he was heard.

Officer Ross turned around to eyeball the jokester before he continued his statement. "Like I was saying…we're here to help prevent any other casualties. I read the whole manuscript, and it isn't clear on stopping catastrophe."

"Casualties are capricious. And you will learn that manuscripts and any other type of book that you have ever read are obsolete when it comes to experiencing the real deal. A book can only offer information about the situation. But once you encounter the ordeal for yourself, all of that book malarkey goes out of the window."

"So, what exactly are you saying?"

"One thing that we must always remember is that in a split second or in the blink of an eye, a situation can be turned in many different ways. We have studied the basics. We know the fundamentals, but that still isn't sufficient. We must expect the unexpected. Stay alert and note that extreme measures manifest desperate causes."

"Any tips on how to control the outcome of a situation?"

"People's minds are congested with evilness these days, so the end results are unpredictable. Every case is different. Therefore, the outcome of every situation will never, ever be the same. But we still have to use our heads. Apply force if necessary. Call for back up. Use reverse psychology. Do whatever you have to do to get the job done. But just get the job done."

Captain Smith peered at his team and decided that he had made an excellent exploitation. He no longer needed to lecture or continue the pep talk. By the expressions on their faces, it was clear he had said at least one thing that registered into their minds.

"Are there any more questions?"

"No," they all sounded off in monosyllables.

"Okay, then. Let's get back to work."

Chapter 4

Asa closed the trunk to her new Ford Fusion after grabbing her large grocery sack. Her cellphone was ringing, but there was no way that she could answer it without having to juggle them all. Fortunately, she decided to wait to answer it at an appropriate time. As Asa was entering the house, someone stood off at a distance, watching her every move. His mouth had been watering ever since he first laid eyes on her at Kroger. This once-sane man had turned ill-minded within a matter of seconds. For some reason, he had to have her. Waiting to play the attraction game just wouldn't do. He had followed her almost subconsciously. But, as he came to, he knew he had to make his move because he came too far to turn back now.

He licked his lips while he stared at her from behind the bushes. In this unknown neighborhood, his ability to think accurately had been altered. He wasn't sure if anybody was watching him or not. Truthfully, none of that mattered. He had come to this exact spot and mustered up a chief purpose, and accomplishing his goal was all that mattered.

By this time, Asa had laid everything down on the table. She grabbed her phone, flipped it open, and scrolled down to her recent missed messages. The last call was from her mother.

"Aw. She's probably just checking up on me," she said to herself. Obviously, she wasn't in a rush to call her mom back because she laid the phone back down on the table and shot toward the back of the house. She went into her bedroom closet, gathered her night clothes and hygiene items, and then went into the bathroom to run her bath water.

The stalker was outside of Asa's house. She didn't know it, but he was watching every move that she made. He followed her from room to room. Occasionally, he peeped through the windows to make sure that no one else was home. After a few minutes of mimicking her movements, his blood began boiling. He had never seen the sight of such a beautiful woman up close before. Her skin was flawless. Her hair was long and shining. Her body was that of a goddess. He was hypnotized while he gazed upon her voluptuous physique. He almost went crazy when she dropped all of her clothes to the floor and stepped inside the shower.

He could no longer control his actions. He began fidgeting and biting his fingernails like he was geeking for some type of illegal drug. He gently slid his hand up the bathroom window. When he realized it was locked, he tried the bedroom window, but it was to no avail. By this time, he was beginning to get frustrated, yet he was determined to get next to this unknown woman. He wasn't leaving until his mission was completed – whatever that was. He quietly moved to the back of house. He nearly knocked over the trashcan because he was awkwardly looking backwards. When he made it to the kitchen window, he noticed that it was smaller than he had thought.

He needed to check the rest of the windows, but he was testing his luck. He used his two thumbs and placed them at both ends of the molding of the window. When he applied a little pressure, the window slid upward, and he automatically rejoiced. There was no stopping him now. He bent the screen that covered the window then removed it to grant him full entrance into the house. He slid the window all the way up then climbed in.

"Shhhh," he said to himself after almost knocking ornaments off the sink. Dishes were piled up on the counter, so he tried his best to move them out of his way without making any noise.

Finally, he was inside the house. He closed the window and looked around. He heard the shower still running, so he tiptoed through the house in case anyone else was present.

"This is a nice house," he admitted. "A really nice house."

He admired all the foreign ornaments, oriental rugs, and Asian vases. For a moment, he wished that it was his home. Besides the dirty pots, pans, plates and utensils in the sink, she was basically a clean person.

The intruder didn't know what he was about to do in this house, but it was too late to turn back. He stood to the side of the door and waited until Asa came out of the bathroom. When she opened the door, she had a large bath towel wrapped around her beautiful body. She started walking directly towards her bedroom.

Before she could make it all the way to the bed, she had a strange feeling. It was like the gravity in the room had changed. For some odd reason, she could feel someone standing behind her. She stopped in her tracks, grasped the towel even tighter, and turned around.

She screamed at the top of her lungs. Being face-to-face with an unfamiliar man made her nervous. She dropped her towel.

"Don't be frightened," he said. "I just want to talk to you."

"Who are you?!" she asked while shaking in her birthday suit. "And what are you doing in my house?"

He reached out to grab her hand, but she yanked it away. He didn't know what his next move was going to be. He was stunned, as if her body were some kind of mental tranquilizer in his brain.

Asa was just standing there, waiting for the outcome of this situation. She gradually started backing up, preparing herself to run. When the intruder realized that she was fleeing, he shouted and ran after her. Suddenly, they were on a high-speed chase. Asa knew her one-room house well. She sprinted towards the living room. As she reached for the doorknob, Stalker Man pushed her arms away. He got a grip on her body, but she somehow managed to get away. He began chasing her around the couch. She zigged and zagged. She was quick – but then again, who wouldn't be if they were terrified for their life. Stalker Man was getting agitated with chasing her around and around. He jumped on the couch, and then hopped over it.

He snagged her delicate frame and pinned her down. She began kicking and yelling. He didn't want the neighbors to hear her, so he covered her mouth with his hand.

She struggled to get up; he was overpowering her. He looked her square in the eyes but didn't pay attention to the well of tears in her pupils. He saw something else. He imagined the beauty beneath the terror. The grace despite the malice.

He was aroused the longer his body laid on hers. The more he wanted her, he began to want all of her. For a moment, he wished that she were actually his. But for now, he would be satisfied with just touching her entire body. He got up on one knee and planted it between her legs. While still applying pressure with the rest of his body, he gripped his hand tightly around her whole face and twisted her neck as if he were telling her in some strange way that if she made any sudden moves or sound, he would rip her neck off.

She whimpered a little bit. She was still petrified and shaking from the horror. She couldn't wait until this event was over.

He began rubbing his hand over the entire length of her body. At times, he only caressed certain special areas. His blood was flowing rapidly, and his erection was harder than an iron bat.

She didn't understand exactly why this man was in her house.

She didn't know what he wanted, yet she suspected during the process of this intrusion that she was about to get assaulted.

He rose up on both knees and unbuckled his pants. She yelled and jerked as an attempt to get up and run. He forcefully yanked her back down and smacked her in the face as hard as he could. The blow immediately sent a chill through her spine.

Now she was ready for submission. He bolted her back into the floor. While she was mute and her body was limp, he took his pants and boxers all the way off. Next, he spread her legs and didn't take any time thrusting his man-parts into her honey pot. He savored every stroke.

Somehow, the best that he ever had was the worst she would ever encounter.

Chapter 5

S o how was your date, Mark?" Shane asked, just to start the day off with a causal conversation. "I must admit that it was alright. It wasn't what I expected it to be, but it went fairly well."

"What did you expect it to be like?"

"I never went out with a chick that had a kid before. Now, don't get me wrong, there ain't nothing wrong with kids, but I always figured that if the father of the child didn't want the girl, then something must be wrong with her."

"Something like what?" Ann broke up their conversation in a defensive manner.

"I meant something like…she's got some type of derogatory attitude, or she's a cheater or compulsive liar."

He tried to sound polite as possible. He didn't want to give off the impression that he was a womanizer in front of a woman.

"Uh-huh…"

"But anyway…like I was saying, Shane, before we was rudely interrupted."

He turned away from Ann in an attempt to tune her out.

"Our date was pretty decent. It was way better than I expected. I thought we was going to have an annoying brat on our hands, but everything went legit. We had fun. Sherie is nice, intelligent, honest, and, as far as I can see, dependable."

"And sexy! Huh?" Ann asserted. She winked her right eye then nodded.

"Yeah. She's incredibly sexy. I can see myself spending a lot of time with her and Marcus."

"That's great," Shane said. "Something that started out as challenge turned into a success."

"You are so right. Todd really looked out for me by putting me up to this task. But the ironic part of the situation is that he don't even know it."

"We'll tell him."

"How has Todd been doing anyway? I haven't seen him in about three days. After hustling him out of one of his off days, plus my two normal off days, I haven't seen the fellow in a while. I kind of miss him."

No one answered Mark's question. Ann began checking out the customers in her line, and Shane ignored him.

"Okay, sir, that'll be fourteen dollars and ninety-five cents."

The Hispanic man dug into his wallet, found fifteen dollars, and then handed them over to Ann. After she accepted the money, he said. "Keep the change."

"Wow!" She exclaimed sarcastically. "A whole nickel. You are so kind. Thank you!"

"No problem," he said, sounding sincere. "I'll do anything for the ladies."

The Hispanic man grabbed his products from off the

counter. He walked out the door with his siblings trailing him.

"Does this fix-a-flat stuff really work?" a young white girl asked the cashier.

Shane grabbed the bottle then turned the can around to the back.

"Just read the instructions before you use it. It's really simple. All you have to do is shake the can well."

He demonstrated by utilizing the can to perform every direction he gave.

"Then place this nozzle on your tires tube, clamp down on the lever, then squeeze this button until the foam inflates your tire."

"It's that easy, huh?"

"Yes, I've used it several times before. As long as your tire doesn't have a huge hole in it, the foam inside the fix-a-flat will seal up any opening in your tire for a long time."

"Thank you," she said. "You was a big help. I like Auto Zone because the atmosphere is so friendly."

"You're very welcome. Drive safe and come again."

"I will."

After Shane rang the total up for the young girl's item, they exchanged currency. He waited until the customer was all the way out the door before he spoke again.

"Now, to answer your question about if Todd is all right..."

"Good," Mark declared. "I thought y'all totally ignored me."

"Nah. It ain't nothing like that. I didn't disregard your question to ignore you. I didn't want to bring up an unpleasant conversation about an employee in front of our customers."

"Yeah. He's right. Listen to him because you may want to hear this before Todd comes back."

Mark was all ears. His attention span stood at full alert. He desperately wanted to know what was going on with his coworker.

"Todd hasn't been himself lately. He's been acting very strange. I'm not sure if he's on some type of medication, illegal substance, or if he's going through some type of unknown crisis in his life. But I'll tell you one thing – the dude has been displaying very suspicious behavior lately."

"I'm worried about him myself," Ann said.

"How suspicious is his behavior?"

"Man, Todd went from normal to creepy in the last couple days. He's cranky and has a nasty attitude. He's been sleeping on the job, and, when I try to wake him up, he's unaware of his surroundings. Plus, the look in his eyes is like he's depressed."

"I'm afraid that, as the general manager of Auto Zone, I'm going to have to fire him. Truthfully, Todd is my friend, and he used to be a good worker. But when it comes down to business, personal affairs have nothing to do with it."

"I understand your position as the manager. But have a heart, man. Todd is our protégé. We have known him for too long. Everyone deserves a second chance. Before you hang him out to dry, at least let me talk to him first. I know all of us are curious to find out what's going on."

"Okay. I'm going to give him another chance." Shane pointed his finger rigidly. "But if he doesn't straighten up and fly right, then I have to let him go."

"All right. I'll handle it. Just give me a little time and be patient. Our workplace will be back to normal, just like the old days."

"Yeah, it had better be because if you don't handle this situation, then I will."

Chapter 6

Captain Smith sat at the table for a long time. He tapped the bottom of his ink pen against the desk until the repetitive noise agitated him. He attempted to relax more by slumping in a downward position in his rolling chair. He placed the ink pen against his temple in an attempt to contemplate more.

He'd been doing research for hours. He graduated at the top of his class from Vanderbilt University. His sociology degree and studies on psychopaths had him trying to figure out what remedies can be taken to avoid further assaults. He thought and thought, but his conclusions were blocked.

"Hey! What are you doing?" Lieutenant Thompson had sneaked up on him. "I was on my way out, but I couldn't help but notice you drooping behind this desk. Is something wrong? Usually you'd be gone by now."

"Nah. I was just sitting and going over a couple of things, particularly the Chad Rosenbeck case, the one that ended in a suicide. I don't seem to understand some of these..."

He thought to himself for a moment, then choked up his next words. "What should I call them? Because they're not humans."

"Freaks. Perverts. Pedophiles. And the list goes on and on with more degenerate names."

"Right." He pointed his finger to indicate that she chose the correct words.

"Do you want to know what I think?"

"Your opinion wouldn't hurt."

"I think that it's not for us to try to understand them. If we try to understand them, then our minds will justify why they do these things to not just themselves but others, also."

"You have an understandable point there. That explains why good cops go bad. Maybe they concentrate on why the bad guys do the bad things so much. They end up seeing themselves doing them. Somehow, a nerve gets struck, and the crimes become justifiable."

"Nah. That's not it at all. Good cops go bad because they want to go bad. They have that bad boy mentally suppressed in them all along. One day it just surfaces, and they act on it."

Miranda and Henry shared a laughed together. Through all of their intense circumstances, they were always able to keep a keen sense of friendship. They had been working side-by-side and experiencing the ups and downs of their careers for so long. They knew what each other's reactions and emotions would be like they were in sync.

Coincidentally, Lieutenant Thompson knew that there was more on Henry's mind than just his case files. Her eyes scanned around the room and noticed his traveling bag was on the floor next to his desk.

"Did you know that being an agent was not part of my original plan?" He asked. "Truthfully, it wasn't even secondary. Becoming an agent was more like a spur-of-the-moment thing. I started off as a super cop turned detective. My detecting record was so impeccable, the FBI decided to offer me a job."

He sighed to himself. "And just to think about it…"

He zoned out like he was reminiscing about a romantic memory. "The only reason why I took the physical at the police academy in the first place was because…"

"Betty got pregnant with your first child," Miranda finished his sentence for him. "I know. I know." She repeated. "You told me that story at least a hundred and one times."

"I'm sorry." He realized that he was in over his head. "I didn't mean to be intruding."

"Aw. It's nothing like that. It's just getting really late, and I have to go in to get prepared for more work tomorrow!"

"Yeah. I guess that I better get some rest, too!"

"All right. I'll see you in the morning." She looked down at his traveling baggage to let him know that she had seen it. "Take care of yourself."

"Okay. I will."

He dragged his respond out before he grabbed his bag then slid it further behind his desk. "Later."

They waved at each other, then Miranda walked away, puzzled.

Chapter 7

Leslie laid in the bed sideways. She had one leg stretched all the way out. The other one was bent at her knee. She knew the exact time that her husband would be entering the door, so she waited for the perfect time to strike a dynamic pose for this remarkable moment. In the back of her head, she wondered what Chuck got her for their anniversary or if he had gotten her anything at all. She took off work early to go shopping around for that magical gift. She ran all around K-Mart, Dillard's, and Home Depot, but she still couldn't find a significant item. She wanted something with a bang to it. Something that would leave a memorable impression. She needed something that meant that their love would be united forever. However, none of those stores had anything that could encompass her message. She sat in the department store parking lot and pondered until she came up with a wonderful idea. She headed straight to Cupid's adult store. Once she got inside the building and saw all of the erotic entertainment, he went crazy with her purchasing.

Now she laid seductively in bed with her new addition from Victoria's Secret. She had some toys tucked under the pillow that she wanted to experiment with, even though her hubby's anniversary gift was on her body. It was mainly for him. The bunny rabbit ears, chains, whips, handcuffs, balls and vibrator were just a little something extra to spice their romance up.

Right on cue, Chuck walked into the house at his normal time. He wasn't ever a minute shy or a second late. If one were asked, they would have to say that he was a peculiar type of guy. He liked for everything to be precise. His motto was: "If you're on time, then you're late." He preferred to be ahead of the game and on top of everything.

When he entered the house, it was always thirty minutes after seven o'clock. The sun had settled down about an hour earlier, and the dark clouds had come creeping through the night. The first thing he did was go into the kitchen and grab a can of beer from the refrigerator. He popped the Miller Light open and took a sip. Next, he opened the oven to see if his wife had left dinner for him. And, like always, there was a plate of fried pork chops, mashed potatoes, green beans and muffins. He placed the plate into the microwave and set it to warm for at least six minutes. After that, he took another sip of his beer and ran upstairs.

"Honey, I'm home!" he sang out in a harmonious melody. "How did your day go?" he asked once he made it into their bedroom.

Leslie didn't respond. She just laid there and google-eyed him.

"You got it smelling really good up in here, babe," he stated, while taking off his work boots and shirt.

"You look different too. What did you do? Did you buy you some more new nighties?" He went into the bathroom to turn the shower on. When he came back out, he had already taken his pants off and tossed them to the side.

"Come over here and have a seat next to me, babe." She patted on a spot next to her in bed. "I have something very special that I want to give to you."

"Hold up. Give me one minute. I'm about to lay next to you. But, before I do, I have to shower and eat. I worked so hard at work today. I know as soon as I lay down, I'm going straight to sleep."

He put his beer can down on top of the nightstand, then ran back downstairs. When he returned to the room, he had his plate in his hand. He grabbed the remote control from the counter and flicked the television on.

Leslie was mentally and sexually frustrated. She felt like he was oblivious. While Chuck sat at the edge of the bed, she stared at him angrily and watched him eat every bite of his meal.

"Chuck..." she said politely, trying to hide her true emotions.

"What is it, honey?" he answered but never turned around to face her.

"Do you know what today is?"

"Uh. It's Monday." He twisted his head around. "Are you all right?"

"Yes, I'm okay. Are you all right?"

"Then, tell me, what's so important about this particular day?"

"It's another day closer to the end of the year. Tomorrow is payday."

He slumped his shoulders.

"We lived to see another day. I don't know what's so important about this particular day. It ain't nobody's birthday. Not that I can recall, anyway."

She laid there, still for a few seconds, until it registered in her head that he truly didn't remember the date that they got married. She was furious, and she was about to lose her mind. She hopped off the bed and smacked him dead in the back of his head. The lick was so hard. Her hand turned red on contact.

"Hey! What did you do that for?" He fumbled with his plate but regained control over it and stabilized it in his lap. "That hurt!" He rubbed the back of his head.

"You didn't even remember our anniversary! We've been married for eight years. That's eight whole years, Chuck, that I spent my life with you." She paced the floor and screamed. "I put these expensive linens on for you. The flowers, the fragrances…the candles were all for you, but you didn't recognize it. What's wrong with you? What is happening to us? Or is there even still an 'us' anymore?"

"I'm sorry, baby. I know that's pretty silly of me to forget our anniversary again. But I've been so busy with work and trying to advance in this company. It's hard on me, and I tend to forget things from time to time. I know you're probably too upset to go out on the town for a casual dinner, but, if you bear with me. I promise that I'll make it up to you."

"You wanna know what's so odd about that statement you just made?"

She hit him upside the head again. She swung one more time, but he ducked and rolled. He left his dinner scattered over the sheets. He then sprinted to the other side of the bed.

"That's the same thing that you said last year on our

anniversary. And the year before that. And then the year before that one, too. I'm sick of it!"

"I'm sorry." He sounded so innocent. "What else do you want me to say?"

"Nothing!" She pushed him out of the way. She was carrying on in a way that no one had ever seen her act out before. She vigorously slid her slippers on her feet and turned around to look her husband up and down in disgust.

Chuck couldn't say anything. He was wrong, and he knew it. Who could possibly appear to have everything in line but miss his own anniversary for four years in a row?

As Leslie stormed past him, she went into the closet and snatched her trench coat from the hanger. She slid each sleeve on her arms and pranced downstairs. By the time that she made it out the door, Chuck was puzzled. He stood there, hopeless and limp, with a dumbfounded look on his face.

This dude been lurking in the park for two whole days now. He was dressed in all black. He had a ski mask on his head, and it was folded above his eyebrows.

It was getting chilly outside, and it appeared to be another long night. Yesterday, he didn't have any luck, and tonight seemed to be a repeat of the day before. He rubbed his hands together and blew steam out of his mouth to warm up. He decided that if he didn't get any action within the next five minutes, he was going to call it a night. Besides, he had already been in the park for hours. Unfortunately, he had to go in early because work would be calling his name before he knew it.

After a few more minutes of leaning against an oak tree,

he thought that he heard footsteps coming his way from a distance. It was quiet in the middle of the night, so any sound would draw attention. He bent down to zero in on the sound. He guessed that the bending and leaning of his ear were going to make it extra silent. And his sense turned out to be accurate.

This person was alone. He expected them to be a female. They were petite with long brown hair. They walked like a woman and were about the same height and weight of a potential woman.

As they got closer, he could tell that she was upset about something. She was mumbling angrily to herself. She had her arms folded across her breasts and moved as if she was infuriated.

He timed it perfectly. At first, he eased back a little so she wouldn't notice him hiding behind the tree. He pulled his ski mask all the way over his face to cover it up. When she passed by, he jumped behind her like Jack the Ripper and muzzled her mouth with his hand.

Leslie was frightened. She bucked like a deer and screamed for help, but he didn't care. There wasn't a residence in sight for at least two miles, so he allowed her to holler all that she wanted to.

He finally got tired of her screaming, so he muffled the sound. She didn't know what was going on or what was about to happen. But the first thing that she did do was make a wish. She wished she was at home with her husband right about then.

After minutes of scuffling with her strong assailant, she realized that she was too frail to fight him off. He had already ripped the buttons off her coat. He even snatched the zipper apart.

By the time he had finished pulling off the leather that covered her threads, he was excited to see that she only had on a thin piece of clothing that dangled from her body. It was easy to slide the hem of her garment up over her waist.

"Wow!" He whispered to himself. She didn't have on any panties, as if she was prepared to be raped.

As he compelled her to stay pinned to the ground, he slid his penis from out of his windbreaker pants. He forced her legs to spread then pushed his little man inside of her and stroked arrogantly until he skeeted. He didn't care about her emotions or feelings. His only concern was reaching a climax. When he was through with her, he got up and walked away. By the time that she recuperated, he would be in his car, long gone and away from the scene.

Chuck waited patiently for his wife to come from out of the bathroom. There had been times that she was in there for a while. But this particular time surpassed all the others.

Truthfully, she didn't even know that he was awake. Because when he heard her come into the house, he played possum. Now he started getting worried. The shower had been running for over two hours, and his beauty still hadn't come out.

He lifted the edge of the blanket off him then slid one leg onto the floor. He silently raised up and contemplated whether or not he should go in the restroom. After minutes of going back and forth with his thoughts, he came to the conclusion that he didn't have anything to lose.

At first, he knocked on the door because he didn't know if she wanted some privacy or not. But, after moments of her keeping quiet, it mad him wonder if something was wrong. Immediately, he opened the door and barged in.

When he found her, she was sitting in the corner of the shower. She was crying and incoherent. He didn't know whether she was trembling because the water was cold or just because she was naked.

"Come on, baby," he said in a soft voice.

He always knew when it was the right time to use courtesy words.

"Everything is going to be all right. We're going to make it through my forgetfulness and unreasonable excuses. I didn't know that I hurt you this bad by forgetting our anniversary, but I vow to make it up to you."

Leslie was convulsing and speechless. Chuck repeatedly tried to touch her, but she wouldn't let him. She flinched every time that he reached his hand out towards her.

"What's wrong, Les? You're not acting like yourself."

He finally realized that something was amiss.

"Talk to me, babe. You can trust me." He talked as if he was now engaging in his feminine side. Chuck couldn't stand to see his wife feeling bad, so he grabbed both of her shoulders.

"Talk to me. You got me worried sick." He looked in her eyes and could sense that she was confused. "It's me!" he yelled. "I'm Chuck. Your husband." He shook her a little bit. "Tell me what's the matter. Please tell me what's wrong!" he begged.

She finally looked up and gazed into his eyes. Her eyes had a well of tears in them. She shook her head from side to side. After a while. She recognized who he was and where she was. She jumped out of the shower and hugged him. She clinged to Chuck so strong that he thought she was a bodybuilder.

"Baby," she cried. "I'm glad you're here for me."

"I will always be here for you. I know that I forgot about our anniversary, but we are going to grow pass that. We invested too many years to let an incident stop us from progressing.

"That's not it!" She wiped a tear from her eye but continued to whimper.

"What is it, then, baby?"

"He...he raped me." She sobbed even some more.

"What? Who did what?"

"When I was in the park earlier..." she told her story slowly. "...a man came up behind me. He held me down and raped me."

Chuck didn't know what to do. He couldn't understand how this tragedy could have come about so quickly. He always watched the news to keep track of the local crimes. He never imagined that something this obscure would happen this close to his home. Especially not to the one he loved. He was fuming.

"We got to do something about this." He paced and forth across the floor. "I'm about to call the local authorities."

Chapter 8

"Y"ou must have had a long night or something," Mark implored, trying to get his homeboy to snap out of the trance he was in.

"Nah! Nah! I'm all right." He sounded frantic. "Why you asked me that?" Todd shook his head from side to side. Anyone who saw him would assume that he wasn't aware of his surroundings.

"You look rough, man. I happened to look over and notice that you was slouched over on the counter with your hand underneath your chin. So, I have to ask you again. Are you a'ight? Because you looked asleep to me."

"Yeah. I'm gucci. Just a little nauseated." He yawned then wiped the slobber from around his mouth. His eyes were bloodshot red. "I don't look too bad, do I?"

"Not really. You don't look that bad, but there's something that I need to talk to you about. I'm going to holla at you later on about it but you need to get yourself together because…"

"Can y'all believe this?"

Shane came from out of the office with some paperwork in his hand. He looked at Mark then at Todd to see if he had their full attention.

"Central office still hasn't approved my vacation. After all the information that I sent them, they haven't respond. And the thing that's wrong with this scenario is that I had made them well aware that I was going to leave Ann as the acting manager while I'm gone. All of the receipts and money drop-offs were going to be verified daily."

Hearing that their coworker was going to be head over them for at least a weekend startled both of them.

"Hold up, wait a minute." Mark held up his hand to stop Shane mid-conversation. "Did I just hear you say that you was gonna leave Ann in charge of us?"

"Yes. You did. I think that Ann is very responsible and a respectful human being. I think that she will operate this store identical to the way that I run it."

Todd and Mark looked at each other in amazement. So many thoughts ran through their minds. They didn't know which choice of words to use first.

"I'm not a hater or anything like that, but I think that you should have picked one of the guys to run the store."

"Why?"

"Because Ann is not the perfect candidate for the position. You just don't know how she plays us when you're not here." Mark was fidgeting. "For one, she's always running late. She's lazy, so all the work is practically thrown on us. And I think that if ya give her a little power, she will abuse that authority."

"Uh-huh!" Shane placed his index finger against his temple. "I see where you are coming from."

"Yeah, man." Todd felt that he had to stress his side of the matter for some unknown reason. "I agree with Mark that you should leave one of the guys in charge, also."

"Todd, you have no right to voice your opinion because you are on thin ice."

"I meant exactly what I said." He used his hand to demonstrate his next statement. "Your job is dangling on a thin piece of thread here at Auto Zone."

"Ever since these white folks let you become manager at this raggedy store…"

"Uh…I don't mean to cut you off in the middle of ya'll's heated conversation, but do you mind if I make an observation?"

"You do know that you're white too, don't you?" He smirked.

"This is not the time for games," Todd scolded him.

"Yeah, Mark," Shane added. "Mind your own business!"

"Like I was saying before I was rudely interrupted… you've been having your head stuck up your butthole ever since these uppity white folks gave you this position. From the first day that you put on that supervisor's seal, you've acted like your stuff don't stank. You must've forgot where you came from." Todd put his finger in Shane's face. "You changed. I remember when we used to be inseparable friends. Now all you do is take everything too seriously." Shane grabbed his finger then quickly pushed it out of the way. "Yeah. Somebody's got to take things serious around here. This is not just my job. This is my career. There's a difference between the two. I'm doing good for myself. By putting bread on the table and paying the bills. And I'll be a plum fool to let anyone get in the way of that."

"So, you're trying to say that I'm jeopardizing your career?"

"I'm saying that I'm not a kid anymore. I grew up a long

time ago. And I think that you need to do the same."

"You know what?"

Todd was pacing the floor back and forth as if he was about to have an anxiety attack.

"I don't have to take this from you."

He grabbed his name badge, snatched it off his shirt, then threw it against the wall.

"I'm more man than you will ever be. You're nothing to me, Shane. You're nothing, and I do mean nothing." Todd got louder as he wrestled his way out of his work shirt. He then slammed it onto the floor.

"I quit!" He barged out the door.

"Do something about that, man," Mark requested. "We just can't let him quit like that."

"Ah. Forget that boy." Shane waved his query off. "I'll have another worker like him by tomorrow. Do you know how many applications that I have in the back? People beg me for jobs every day."

Mark stared at him in disbelief." You just don't understand, do you?" He ran out the door and flagged Todd down before he got into his Nissan Maxima.

"What's up? What you want, dawg?" He sat down in his vehicle but left one of his legs on the outside of the car.

"I need to holla at you."

Todd looked up at Mark like he really didn't want to hear what his coworker had to say, but they had been best friends for so long. He figured that he at least owed him the respect to hear him out.

"Please don't quit."

"Pshhh." Todd held his hand out so Mark could step away from the car. Then he began to close the door. "I don't need this rubbish."

Mark snatched the door back open before he could look at it. "Look! That's what Shane wants you to do. So, if you quit, then you're playing right into his hands. Now, come on. I know you're smarter than that."

"I just can't take these weird looks and vulgar language that this guy be giving me no more. Lately he's been catching an attitude like a little female. And all this time, I thought we was supposed to be better than that."

"Forget about Shane. Don't let another man's actions dictate what you do and don't do. You owe it to your family to keep on working. And truthfully...you owe it to yourself not to give up on yourself."

"You're right, man. I'm not gonna quit because I got a lot going on for myself. Besides...I'll be giving that sucker an easy way out.

"So, what you say?" Mark motioned his hands towards the store. "You coming back in or what?"

Todd stepped out of the car and slammed the door. He reached over and grabbed Mark's shoulder and whispered, "Don't tell nobody, but I'd prefer for him to fire me. Because if I quit, then I can't get an unemployment check."

"Now you're thinking."

After the duo re-entered Auto Zone, Shane gave them a cold stare. Todd didn't pay him any attention. He picked his shirt and name badge from the floor then went behind the counter.

"I guess you have decided to stay for the time being," Shane said. "But I guarantee you that it won't be for too much longer. I got plans for you, boy!"

Chapter 9

Yeah. Girl, you just don't know how bad I hate being on the night shift." Denise rotated the phone to the other ear so that her right hand could move freely."

"I can't say I know how you feel 'cause I ain't never worked graveyard before. But I can say that everything seems like it's working out the best for you."

"And what do you mean by that, Catrice?" She asked, while placing several items into the bag she opened.

"All I'm saying is that if you was working the same shift with me, then who'll be keeping your baby?"

"Yeah." She dragged her voice. "I guess you right 'bout that one."

"Think about it. If you was on the first shift with me, then we wouldn't be able to get nothing done," Catrice added. "I mean it's cool and all that, we got hired on the job at the same time before they divided us up like this. That's the best thing that ever happened."

"And how's that?" She inquired with a snobbish attitude.

"When I'm asleep, you're awake to take care of my business. But when I'm off, I can keep Danny boy for you."

"We is a team, ain't we?"

"Most definitely. But speaking of Danny boy, when was the last time you seen that child's father?

"His daddy need to be keeping him some time so I can take a break."

"I haven't seen that no good negro in about three weeks. The only time he comes over here is when he thinks he going to get some pooh-nanny from me." Denise smacked her luscious lips. "Then he be coming over here with teddy bears and junk trying to play the daddy role. But this coo-coo down there is locked tight. I learned my lesson; the next guy that gets between these legs better be a potential husband."

"I know that's the truth!"

The two girls giggled together at each other's comments.

"Hold up." Denise got serious for a moment.

"What's up?"

"I guess thought about what you said. I know you ain't talking about taking no break from keeping my child. I don't be saying nothing about taking no breaks when you be having me run all around this city paying your bills and buying your groceries."

Catrice laughed off her sister's statement. "I was kidding with you, girl. I love my nephew."

"You better…because he sho' loves you."

"While we're talking about my nephew…how long will it be before I see the lil' fellow?"

"I'm about to get ready and walk out of the door now. We'll be over there in five minutes, so you better not be sleep."

"How you getting to work tonight?"

"The same way I always do, of course. When I drop Danny boy off, I'll walk to the bus stop that's down the street from your house."

"Do you mean to tell me that you still haven't found you a hunk of a man to drive you to work on a daily basis?"

"Chile, please…I don't use men for rides, and I'm most definitely not a car whore."

"Call it what you want, but you guts to make something happen."

"This discussion is over with. I'll see you in five minutes." Denise hung the phone up on her sister then put the Blackberry in her pocket. She turned to glance at her child, who was still sound asleep in his stroller. She then finished filling the diaper bag with bottles, Pampers, toys, baby wipes, and a pacifier.

After she made sure all was well, Denise made her way through each room in her house to cut the TVs and lights off. She walked out of the house and locked the door. She used caution to motion the wheels on the stroller down the stairs gently. Denise was a young, black, and beautiful woman. Every inch her five-foot-four frame was godly. But what complemented her the most was her smooth skin. The Vince leather mini skirt that she sported exposed her toned calf muscle.

The dark clouds glazed perfectly over the night sky. Even though it wasn't exactly in the wee hours of night, it was smart to get into one's house as soon as possible. After three minutes of walking, she began to feel uncomfortable. At first, she thought it was because of the late hours, but then again, she walked this same path a hundred times and never felt jumpy before.

For a moment, she shook it off, but with every other step she took, the creepy feeling came back to haunt her, as if she was in some type of horror movie.

For a minute, she began hearing footsteps, and she was frightened. Denise didn't want to try running because she figured that it would create suspicion.

She decided since she was only a few blocks away from her sister's house, she would act normal. But the closer she got to her destination, the footsteps sped up and were definitely closer. She could almost hear the person breathing. She kept moving, but she had to stop momentarily to pull the blanket back over her son, who was still asleep in the stroller.

After she was finished attending to her son, she unintentionally peered behind her on instinct. She subconsciously wanted to see who this mysterious person was. Contrary to her belief, the person had disappeared. She thought that maybe he had turned off onto another street or possibly gone into one of the many houses that they passed by.

By the time she leaned forward to push the stroller ahead, she saw a shadow moving in her peripheral vision. The shadow was coming in her direction at full speed. Her gut was telling her that something was wrong. The first thing that came to her mind was to protect her child. She bent over and wrapped her arms around the entire stroller. The second thing that overpowered her was fear.

The masked man saw the submission in the young black girl. He knew at that moment that his mission was going to be easy for the night. He slowed down a few feet before he was directly in the girl's face. She was shaking nervously, and for some reason he liked the horrific power that he acquired.

"What's wrong?" she asked with a trembling voice, not want to look up directly into this human's eyes.

He didn't respond. He only continued to walk closer to her.

"What you want?" Her voice got louder.

The masked man pulled out a short knife with a shiny blade on it. By the look in Denise's eyes, you could tell that it was sharp.

"I don't have any money," she confessed then began taking off her accessories. "I promise I don't want any problems. Here, you can have this." She held out her four-teen-carat gold necklace and ring. "Just take it and leave us alone."

The masked man shook his head no. He then walked around the petrified lady and put his hand over her mouth. All Denise could think about was the well-being of her child. He twirled the knife around her face then placed it on her neck.

"I'll give you whatever you want." She said, muffled. "Just don't hurt me or my baby."

He remained silent. He used one hand to keep the blade to her throat. With his free hand, he reached around to the front of her skirt and moved his fingers up to her most valuable possession.

Denise had never had a sharp object held to her body by an aggressive villain before. Words couldn't explain the ways she felt. All she could do was whimper while an unknown predator slid her panties down in the middle of the sidewalk.

"Please don't do this to me," she begged. "Please stop."

Denise tried to move his hand, but he instantly became more aggressive. At that moment, she knew that this infidel was going to have things his way or no way at all. She didn't want to cause alarm by screaming because he might just slit her throat.

In a situation in which one must choose between two evils, it is always wiser to pick the lesser evil. So, with that being innate into her head, she did what she had to do. And that was negotiate.

"Okay," she cried out. "If you gonna do this, please don't do it in front of my child. At least have the dignity and respect not to do it in front of my child. He's only a baby," She whined.

The masked man was hesitant momentarily. She must have said something that struck a nerve in him. He stood there and thought to himself before he snatched her by the arm. He led her to the back of what looked like a sleeping resident's house. He didn't waste any time to bend her big ol' juicy butt over and rip her panties off. While he rammed every inch of his manhood into her, Denise cried. She couldn't wait until it was over with so she could get back to her abandoned child.

Chapter 10

Mark leaned back in the colorful couch and almost sunk in. He wrapped his arm around his girlfriend. He had to admit, Sherie didn't have a lick of taste in decorating, but she knew how to please her man. "What's up, babe, why you looking like that?"

"Aw. It ain't nothing much. I'm just tuned into the news channel. There have been some strange things happening around the city lately. For some reason, the crime rate has risen."

"Yeah. I've been noticing the violence, too, so I know what you mean. Nashville used to be called Cash, but I guess folks ain't been getting money no more." She stretched one of her legs out then placed it onto the table. Next, she leaned in closer to snuggle up with her boo thang.

Then they heard a startling beeping sound. They looked around to see what it was. But by the time they found out what it was, it was too late. The remote control SUV had already stampeded into Sherie's ankle.

"Boy! What you think you doing?" She yelled after she jumped up. "You better watch where you going with that yellow truck. You gonna hurt somebody."

"I'm sorry, Momma. I didn't mean it. It won't happen no mo," Marcus promised with a guilty look on his face.

"Come 'ere, lil' man. Let me holla at you." Mark couldn't help but feel sympathy for the lad. Marcus had that type of look on his face that a sane person couldn't resist empathizing with.

Like an obedient child, Marcus complied with Mark's command. He walked up on him with his remote controller still in his hand.

"Come on up here." He motioned for him to hop onto the couch. "Now what seems to be the problem with your vehicle?"

"I don't know it. It was going really fast, so I couldn't stop it. But when I tried to turn it into another direction, so wouldn't it wouldn't hit momma, it lost control."

"So, you didn't mean to hit your momma?"

"No." He sighed sadly. "That's why I blew the horn before it reached her."

"Give me your controller so I can show you something."

After Marcus handed over his transmitter, Mark said, "Look. The vertical switch here is to make your Hummer go forward and backward. But be careful because the longer you hold it, the faster it will go, and it may get out of your control. You already know that the horizontal switch is to make it turn left or right. But here's the catch. When pull this lever downward, it will immediately stop."

"Aw, okay." The child seemed excited to learn something new. "I see what you are talking about."

"Good. Now let me see you try it." After Mark's demonstration, he gave the remote controller back to the kid.

Marcus was a smart kid. He quickly learned the new skill that his friend performed for him. He played with the SUV in front of his mother to show her that he now had his problem subdued. He was happy to wheel the vehicle across the carpet. He sped the Hummer up then stopped it instantly. He did this for minutes until he raced the truck all the way into the back room.

Mark glared over at Sherie. He had an expression on his face that insinuated that he was the man.

"I'm proud of you!" she declared. "That's the type of man I like."

"What kind?" He used his deep, sexy voice.

"One who knows how to diffuse a volatile situation."

"Aw. It ain't nothing." He blushed, really admiring his brownie points.

"Oh, yeah, it was something. You did the right thing. Because I promise you I was about to take that truck form that boy."

"Well I'm glad that I could help."

Mark leaned back into the couch, and Sherie cuddled up with him like before. They resumed watching TV.

Within seconds, the regular news station was interrupted with a breaking news broadcasting. What they were reporting must have been important because big red bars came across the screen with an alarming noise.

Claudia Barr came on the screen saying, "We're sorry to interrupt your local program. But I'm live at the scene where a young African American girl was recently raped hours ago." She began walking the street, and the camera man followed her. "As you can see, this appears to be just an ordinary neighborhood. But we feel it necessary to go public because of the frequency of rapes reported in the last two months."

Mark and Sherie glanced at each other awkwardly then

tuned back into the news broadcasting.

"Recently, in this exact spot, a twenty-seven-year-old, black female was raped. We have the police report, and it appears that she was with her child, which makes the police even more attentive to this case. However, we must also note that there have been a series of rapes, particularly on the East side of Nashville. We're not sure if these rapes are linked to each other at this time. But my guess would be that they are."

"Man, who does this type of thing?" Sherie asked. "Not only did this monster molest this girl, but he took advantage of her in front of a child. I don't even know the girl, but I'm infuriated for her."

"I know what you mean. I despise womanizers. Whoever the coward is needs to be caught and given a life sentence in the toughest prison in the world."

"A life sentence?" she yelled. "Nah. Forget that. That sucker doesn't need to live. Let's not forget that he did this in front of a kid. That dude deserves the death penalty for his crime."

"You're right. The government needs to fry his brain. But the only thing about that is when they place him in the electric chair and strap him down, they need to forget to soak the sponge that goes on top of his head."

"What if the sponge doesn't get soaked?"

"It is there to absorb the smoke while his brain is cooking. For instance, it's like if you put some raw meat in a skillet and turn it on without any water or oil. The meat wouldn't cook properly. It'll burn and possibly set a fire. Smoke will be everywhere.

"Really?"

"Yeah. It'll be the same with the electric chair. If they don't soak that sponge, that machine that's on top of his head will fry his brain, skin, and skull. Sparks of fire and smoke will be jumping everywhere."

"Ooooh! That sounds really horrible."

"You see. That's the thing with females."

"What?" She asked.

"A minute ago, you was talking about how this fellow deserves to die. Now you done got all mushy on me talking about that that's horrible how the government murders people. If you gone be hard then stay hard. Don't start getting all sensitive and soft on me."

"But that do sound bad. He deserves to die. I just wouldn't want to see no one meet their demise like that."

"One thing I know for certain is that as long as he doesn't cross paths with you he'll be all right with me. But if anyone on this earth violates you, they'll have to deal with me."

"Aw. That's so sweet." She rubbed her finger smoothly down his cheek. "Not only do I have a man who's lovable and confident, but he is also a protector."

Mark held her and suggested. " You better be aware when you go out in them streets. I don't want anything happening to you or Marcus."

"I will," she agreed then buried her head into his chest.

Chapter 11

This is living, ain't it, amigo?" Carlito asked, as he raised his beer can to the sky. "Yeah, you right," Mario responded in his Spanish accent. He then toasted cans with his friend. "It can't get no better than this, soldado. We got the women, booze, cars, houses, money and partying with the gamberros."

"Now that we are the general and lieutenant of Seventeen, things will began to run a whole lot smoother now."

"I'm with you, my brother. Seventeen will be known as the most notorious gang throughout all of Tennessee."

"Remember. It ain't always about ruthlessness. We only do what is necessary. If it is mandatory that we have to send out a message to a particular organization, then we do just that. But if it's not necessary then we read the situation right. We don't need any heat coming down on us that we can prevent."

"I read you loud and clear, boss," Mario agreed. He looked around the area and saw his many foot soldiers having fun.

They were Mexicans deep-stretched out across three lawns. Music was playing so loudly that it could be heard over five blocks away, yet no one dared to alert the authorities.

Seventeen was respected and well-established in the

neighborhood. Not only that – they were out for their community. They created jobs and gave out turkeys and presents every Christmas and Thanksgiving day.

"Carlito!" Aleena called out, but she was intentionally ignored. She decided to call his name again.

"¿Que pasa?" he reluctantly asked.

"I'm bored."

"What?" He was caught off-guard. The crinkles in his face expressed that his sister was being obnoxious. "How can you be bored?"

"I just am, okay?" she replied snobbishly. "I can't wait 'til this stupid party is over with."

"That's the problem with you mamacitas. You don't know how to loosen up. We got drinks, food, good music, and games at this party. For Christ's sake."

He held out his beer can and pointed it at different individuals. "Get out and mingle with some of the important people who are here."

Call the time. It's the same ol' thing." She folded her arms across her chest. "I'm tired of these people and parties. I'm tired of living the life of a dough boy's sister. Ever since Papi and Mami got killed in that car wreck, you've been overprotective of me. The only thing that I want to live a normal life."

"Aleena, I do what I have to do to take care of mi familia and make sure we are secured. The way that we live is practically a normal life. The only exception is that we are on a bigger scale than others." He looked over at his homie and could tell that he was engaged in a serious conversation.

"Carlito!" Aleena yelled out. "I'm sitting here pouring my heart out to you, but you ain't even paying attention to me."

"I am paying attention to you," he lied. "You are my baby sister."

"No, you not," she cried. "Everything has to do with you."

Carlito was about to answer his younger sister, but Mario walked up on him with the phone still to his ear.

"Excuse me, general, but we have a problem that needs immediate attention."

"Say, brother," he said aggressively. "Don't you see that I got a situation going on right here? Why would you rudely interrupt us like that?"

Mario didn't want to respond too quickly to his boss's comment. He took a moment to square him in the eyes. After he knew that he had gained Carlito's humility, he reached over and whispered some words into his ear. Whatever he said must have been shocking because the two appeared stunned.

"I will be right back, Aleena," Carlito said in his heavy accent.

"Forget you. You don't ever want to listen to me." She brushed forcefully passed her brother.

He grabbed a strong hold of her arm. "Where do you think you're going?"

"Let me go!" She snatched her arm away. "I'm about to take a walk."

"You ain't going nowhere. It's dangerous out there in those streets. You must have not been watching the news. There's a serial rapist on the loose."

Aleena ignored him. She continued to storm down the road.

"Hey! We're not through with this discussion."

"You don't have to worry about her," Mario assured him. "Everybody in this neighborhood knows that she is your sister. And believe me when I say this – no one wants to deal with the repercussions and consequences of going against Seventeen."

Carlito raised his eyebrow in agreement. On that note, they went to their vehicle and drove away. Aleena jumped at the sound of Mario's loud pipes passing by her. She thought that they were coming to snatch her little body inside the monster truck, but luckily, they didn't. They kept cruising, which was odd to her. She finally figured that something must been really amiss.

She kept walking until she was nearly out of the neighborhood. Aleena didn't normally go anywhere by herself. All her life, she was pampered. She had recently enrolled at Fisk University. She was used to being around girls like herself – the high society ones with no need for face lifts because they were born beautiful.

As Aleena continued to stroll around the unknown area, she tried to think of fond memories. She thought and thought until she began to smile at the times of her beauty pageant days. Of course, her mom and dad were still living then. They wouldn't dare miss an audition.

Walking made her more relaxed. As her anger began to simmer down, she watched the sunset and enjoyed the cool, breezy day. Aleena stopped for a minute to massage her aching calf muscles. She started to turn around and go back home, but she figured she should enjoy the exercise while it lasted. She slowed her stroll down while she passed by a man who was standing still. His back was turned away from her, so she couldn't see his face. By the time she stepped in front of him, he grabbed her around the neck then wrapped a towel tightly around her mouth. She wrestled, but the smell of alcohol had her unconscious within minutes.

The unknown bandit pulled her by the legs until they were behind some bushes. He stared at her for a minute because he was unaware of what he had captured. Sure enough, he knew she was the female because he had followed her for three or four blocks. When he saw the opportunity to get ahead of her, he did just that. Now he had his victim. The bloodthirsty human was astonished like when a cat catches a mouse by his paws. Except he didn't want to eat her. He merely wanted to take her innocence. He took his time to rub his knuckles against her facial features. After snapping out of his trance, he hastily unbuckled her pants and pulled them off, along with her panties. He admired the neatly-trimmed hairs on her crotch. She looked good and smelled nice. He assumed that he was about to have fun with this one.

He eagerly grabbed his thing from out of the windbreaker and primed up. He threw her legs wide open then kneeled down to enter her. Once he was inside, her opening only accepted the head part. He tried to dig deeper, but the passage was blocked. He contemplated to himself for a while before he figured the reason out.

Wow, he thought. She must be a virgin. I hit the jackpot. Yes!

He now grinned as he engaged in the non-consensual sex. The more he stroked, the further he climbed inside of her. By the time he reached his climax, the skin on his penis was ripped. And, for some unknown reason, he thought that she enjoyed the encounter because she had gotten wet. But what the fool didn't know was that the moisture was blood. Luckily, only half of his rod was able to fit in the entire time. But he didn't care. He got what he came for. He slid his bloody pecker back into his pants and left the scene.

Little Aleena was still knocked out. She laid butt-naked in the grass, not knowing if she would awake herself from the bodily fluids that were getting cold or if someone would find her.

Chapter 12

Both lines were packed at the checkout counter. Traffic had been flowing in and out of the double doors all day. The building was warmer and noisier than normal. "Why haven't you said more than two words to me?" Ann imposed.

Mark shrugged his shoulders.

"If you know anything about me, then you would know that I'm going to make you talk to me. So, you might as well give in sooner than later." Ann stopped her harassment to attend to a customer. When she was through, she got back on her coworker's row. "Now tell me what I did to you for you to give me the cold shoulder? You used to be so cute to me, but your attitude stank. Hmph. Giving me the silent treatment like that."

"Is it getting on your nerves?"

"Yes!"

"Well, I'm going to keep doing it, then."

"Aw. Come on, man. Don't be like that. You making the day so hard for the both of us."

Mark smiled. He enjoyed taunting Ann. She was so easy to annoy. "It ain't no hard feelings. I was just tired before this busy day began."

"Mark, how long have you been working here now?

What, like, maybe five or six years. You know like I know that it's always busy on the first and the fifteenth of every month."

"Yeah. I know." He sighed shamefully. "I just had a long night."

"That's your fault, then. You need to learn how to climb up out of that new girlfriend of yours. And go to sleep early." She smiled.

"Now there you go. All up in my business." He said playfully. "You only mad because I ain't never offered to climb up in you."

"Boy. Please!" She brushed him off." You ain't handle this." She popped her hips to make her butt jiggle. "I'm have you sprung out!"

"You wish."

Ann gave Mark a flirtatious look after a patron dressed in red, white, and blue checked out of her line.

"Yeah. It's all good." Shane detoured a young woman towards the cash register. "You don't have to be embarrassed. I have this type of thing happening all the time at the store."

"I'm so sorry if I'm too much trouble," the female with make-up piled on her face said. "I've never had car trouble before, and I want to get this right."

"Like I said before, it's my job to work the floor and make sure my customers is happy. It's no big deal, really. Mr. Mark here can assist you with any further problems."

Mark shook the girl's frail hand and asked, "What seems to be the issue here?"

"I went to a shady mechanic because I don't have much money." She flounced her hand around as she explained her situation.

"Now. I know you looking at me like 'why would you go to a shady mechanic?'. Duh! I know. That's crazy, huh? My fault. But I've been short on funds 'cause I just moved into a new house. Oh yeah! And, by the way, it's a nice crib. I mean, it's really, really, really nice." She took a deep breath. "That's the slang term you guys use for houses nowadays, isn't it? Cribs. Aw. Well." Her wrist danced through the air while making unusual faces. "I went to pay my bills, and unbeknownst to me, while I'm driving down the street, my car shuts off. First, it started rocking from side to side then it made this weird sound like click-click-bang boom-boom."

Mark looked strangely at the lady, who was suddenly out of breath from speed-talking. He didn't want to say much. He immediately glanced over at Shane, who in return had an expression on his face like, "Now you see what I was dealing with. That's why I brought her to you."

"Excuse me, miss. Um, I'm not trying to interrupt your brief story, but can you please just tell me what you need to buy from this store?" He placed his hand on top of his head in disbelief.

"Aw. Okay. I didn't mean to annoy you. I tend to do that sometimes…you know, annoy people because I'm very talkative. They got a word for that. It's called loquacious."

"Ma'am. I'm not trying to be rude right now." He shook his head. It took all the might that he had to keep his temper down. "But yes! You are very loquacious."

Even though Shane was the manager and he knew that customers came first, he laughed at the sight of Mark's meekness.

"I'm sorry. Sometimes I do get out of line." She admitted. "But what I came up here for was an alternator."

"Hold up. Wait." He decided to enjoy himself. "You were back here in the aisles looking for an alternator. That's the funniest thing that I've ever heard."

Shaneice looked at Mark as if he was the idiot now.

"You can't find items like that in the aisle. We have to retrieve that from the back of the store."

"Why?" She asked, fully sassy.

"We have to know the make and model of your vehicle so we can match it to the right part. If it was in the aisle, then you wouldn't understand the numbers on the pieces, so that means we would be having hundreds of customers coming back to return their wrong purchase."

"A'ight, then. I have a 1992 Ford Mustang."

After Mark found the girl's car part, he checked her out then watched her strut her tiny hips from out of the store. Before he knew it, another woman was standing in front of him, ready to be serviced.

"Is this all that you need, ma'am?" He asked, then grabbed the car air freshener oil and WD-40.

"Yes, it is," she responded, then reached inside of her purse to grab her Visa card.

"Your total comes to thirteen dollars and fifty-three cents." He took the debit card then slid it through the machine. It wouldn't scan. He looked at the card to make sure it was on the correct side to be scanned. He then slid it through the machine again. "Ma'am, I'm sorry, but the system isn't accepting your debit. Perhaps you have insufficient funds."

"No, honey! There's nothing insufficient about me or

mines," the older lady said flamboyantly. "Perhaps your system is backed up and you need to try it again and again until you get it right."

"Okay. Whatever you say, I'll scan it one more time, but I'm not about to be standing here all day for you." He slid it through the machine, and by the time the plastic reached the end of the connector, it registered. "Well, what do you know?" He smiled." Your card does work. Your total is $69.32"

"Thank you, honey!" The woman really thought that her husband had cleared their bank account out doing some part in their recent separation. "I didn't mean to be rude earlier. Please forgive me. I just got a little nervous."

"Are you going to be all right?" Mark asked as he sacked up her products then handed it to her.

"I sure hope so. I've been watching the news lately, and they got this rapist on the loose around this area of Nashville."

"Yeah, I saw that, too. You will never know how real drama gets until it hits home."

"I know, right? That's why I'm in such a rush to get home." She grabbed her bag then left the store.

"Man, what a coincidence that was!" He seemed baffled.

"What's the problem?" Shane wanted to know.

"I was just thinking about that same rapist who's on the loose before that woman said something about him."

"Why are you so concerned? You think he want some of your lil' booboo?" Shane jokes. "I don't think that guy into boys, so you have nothing to worry about."

"Naw. It's not like that." He brushed Shane's taunting off. "You know Sherie?"

"The girl you recently started talking to. Am I correct?"

"Yes. Well, she works at a battered women's shelter. Her job is to co-counsel with the ladies who have been tortured, abused, and raped. She doesn't tell me all the details, but I believe that she has begun mentoring the women that this serial rapist has molested."

"How you figure that?"

"Because she said her supervisor recently put her in charge of a special group that just started. Plus, I can tell how emotional she gets when the news mentions that the guy is still at large. Her whole mood instantly saddens."

"Do you think she is getting too attached to the women?"

"Maybe!"

"That's not good. It's okay to have a heart, but in cases like that, you have to know how to keep your relationship strictly professional. Mixing work with home is sure to have an outcome of disaster."

"I know, man. Believe me, I know!"

Chapter 13

"Federal Bureau of Investigation," the clerk answered the phone in the sophisticated manner she was trained in.

"Yes. This is Chuck, and I've been sitting here for weeks watching this insane prank on the news for too long."

"Excuse me. Do you know who you've called, sir?"

"Of course I do. That's why I called." He sounded angry and sarcastic at the same time. "This the FBI, ain't it?"

"Unfortunately, yes. How may I help you sir?" she continued in her low, soothing voice.

"I just told you – women! – Y'all haven't caught the bastard who is running around the great city of Nashville. I'm sure you've heard of the guy. The one who's ruining all of these ladies' lives.

He was loud. "It's only been on every news station in the country. I believe this chump may be prominent worldwide."

"Sir, I'm going to first ask you to calm down. I'm trying to make sense of what you are saying. But I can't because your high-pitched voice is frantic in my ear."

"That's because I'm hysterical." Chuck's redneck accent really kicked in then. "Shhh. You haven't been through what I've been through these last past weeks. My wife can't even sleep. All she does is whimper all night."

"Is the problem with you or your wife, sir?"

"Both!" He screamed at the top of his lungs. "My wife was raped by this masked man who has been treading throughout the city. And you people haven't done anything about it in months."

"Excuse me, sir. This is the FBI. Maybe you need to first report your situation to the local authorities."

"You're such a genius!" He berated sarcastically. "We've already done that. And they haven't given us closure. That's exactly why I'm going a step higher by calling you."

"Well, that's not really how our procedure works here. We have protocols—"

The operator's statement was cut off by Chuck's rude expletives. "I'm so sick and tired of you ******* people. Steadily giving me the run-around."

The clerk took the phone off her ear and stared into the receiver. She couldn't believe the words coming from the other end of the line.

"I got political ties in this ******* town." He never stopped being belligerent when she placed her ear back to the phone. "If you don't let me speak to the ******* person who is over you, then I will make sure that you don't ever have a job again. You got that, you *****?"

It just so happened that Captain Smith was walking out the door and noticed the clerk had put the phone on her desk while shaking her head.

The bureau wasn't set up like any other organization. It had floors on top of floors and levels that even most workers didn't know existed. When Chuck had called, he had gotten through the main directory. Her station was the entry of the front door. It was a nice non-cubicle area, elegant enough to match the marble floors and spectacular walling. Now every level had its own division. And each one carried anywhere from one to three separate secretaries. However, the main section was where she was located. She took on tasks for the Homicide, SWAT, Bomb Squad divisions, and so on.

"What's wrong, Pearl?" Captain Smith asked the receptionist.

Her face was rosy red, and even if you didn't know her, you could still tell that she was embarrassed. Pearl didn't say much. She just pointed towards the phone and frowned.

"Hello?" He aggressively picked up the phone and announced himself in his unexpected voice.

"Who is this?" Chuck stood his ground. "This better be someone with some high rank." He wasn't backing down. "Like I told that elderly lady, I've got political ties in this town, man. And I will have you out of a job if you don't cooperate."

"Okay. All that is fine and dandy, but the first thing we're going to need is for you to calm down. That is, unless you want to hear a dial tone."

Pearl snickered on the other side. Chuck was quiet for a moment. He couldn't believe that a person still didn't comply to his terms. He sat there and pondered this, but a comment couldn't register in his head.

Smith knew he had him where he wanted him now. He was well-trained in dealing with perplexing situations. It's not always good to be demanding when someone is the aggressive type. And it's not always appropriate to use kind words when someone else is stirred up either. It is best to know how to weigh out your options. Mr. Smith didn't become captain by not knowing what to do.

"Now that I have your undivided attention and you are willing to contain yourself, I will try, on behalf of the bureau, to apply our protocols to your problem."

"All I'm saying is that some other type of organization has to take over these catastrophes that are happening in the metro area." He was now very humble. "My wife was a victim of this guy that the media has labeled a serial rapist. I'm sensing that this case has become immense. The FBI should get involved like they do with terrorists and serial murders."

"I understand where you are coming from, sir, but you have to recognize that we choose our own cases to look at. The public doesn't choose them for us. If we went around doing what everybody else wanted us to do, then we would be working 24/7, 365 days a year. We wouldn't ever get any sleep."

"Well, I know one thing. Y'all get paid enough not to sleep."

He chuckled at Chuck's comments. "Is there anything else that I could assist you with?" The Captain looked at Pearl and winked his eye.

"No! That's the only matter that I have. I will tell you one thing, though. If I don't get any aid from the FBI. Then I will have this conversation all over the news media worldwide!"

Smith was stunned. Had he been out-foxed? He knew it was time to get serious now. "Excuse me, sir. What did you just say?"

"Yeah. You heard me. I bet I got your attention now, don't I?" Chuck's temper flared back up. "Just like your bureau automatically records conversations. Well, so do I!" he yelled in the captain's ear before he hung up.

Smith looked at the phone and twisted it from side to side before he placed it on the hook. "Okay, that seemed to go well. What do you think, Mrs. Pearl?"

All the receptionist could do was smile. She loved it when a brave young man took control of a situation, especially a dilemma that could have turned out fatal.

Chapter 14

"What it do? What tha business is?" Ann entered through the door using her hip-hop voice.

"Well, ain't you jelly today?" Shane joked. "Coming in here, throwing your hands up like you some type of gang-banger."

"Nah, I'm just chilling. Ya know what I'm saying?" She grabbed her crotch and pulled up on her pants like she was a man.

Ann was always the life of the store. The vibe instantly changed from the moment of her entrance. No matter where she was, even from youth. At schools, church, home or work, her presence alone was charismatic.

"Nah. I don't know what you saying." Shane imitated her gestures and slang.

"Mane, why you trying to copy me? Jacking my swag and stuff. You sound like an imposter."

Shane laughed hard. He enjoyed taunting her. Even though, the rest of his coworkers were long-term friends. She was his favorite. He glared at her while she passed by him. The store didn't seem too busy that day. After all, Ann always came in late. She was like the only white girl in the whole city of Nashville who didn't get to work on time. She put her bags in the back office before she clocked in.

"Okay now! You can get off my cash register, Shane," she announced once she came back.

Shane didn't hesitate to move away. He raised his hands then chimed, "I got work I have to get caught up on, anyway!"

"Okay, then, hold up, Papi. Chow!" She threw the deuces up at him. "Come chat with me later. I have to tell you about this wonderful apartment in the heights that I'm planning on getting."

"A'ight. No problem!" He replied happily, shrugging his shoulder so Ann would pay attention to her coworker.

Todd was bent over, looking lazily at the cash register beside her. His eyes were halfway shut. He smelled and appeared as if he'd been awake for days.

"What's wrong with you, Todd?" she asked. "You seem like you wired up?"

On cue, Shane walked to his back office.

Todd peeped the play. He caught their manager walking off and just knew Shane had coerced her into filling in the gaps of his incognizance.

"Nah. I'm good." He sighed.

What he was really saying in his head was: They actually expect for her to be late. And with no disciplinary actions at all. Let that shoe be on the other foot. They have sent me out on the first infraction – smoking. I just can't get it. Why does this broad always get to come in late but has never even once been threatened about being fired, yet this so-called boss writes me up for the smallest things I do?

"Todd!" she screamed. "Are you okay?" She laughed it off this time. "You really went into another zone on me just then."

"This will be all I need, people," someone said, a raspy voice interrupting their shenanigans.

They glared around as a car seat cover hit the counter. At first Todd and Ann thought that they both were tripping out because they heard a voice speaking but didn't see anybody.

"This should cover the price for those." The person threw a twenty-dollar bill on top of the counter.

Todd still didn't see a face. He only saw small hands when the money was released onto the counter. He thought it was either an underage child paying or the item or somebody was crawling on the floor to play a game. "I don't mean any harm, sir, but can you take step backwards so I can see you?"

A fully-grown man took two steps backwards. He was every bit of three feet and nine inches. He had a lot of weight on him compared to his size, with a big head but tiny shoes. The dwarf looked up at Todd then threw up his stumpy arms like he was at a concert.

"What? Who has something funny to say?"

Neither Ann nor Todd was in the mood to be sarcastic. They were more amused than anything. Todd grabbed the man's seat cover then scanned them. He didn't want to draw more attention than necessary, so he kept as little eye contact as possible.

Ann being the blunt and inquisitive person that she was, she couldn't contain herself. "Sorry, sir, but excuse me!"

The dwarf smiled. He loved receiving attention from women.

"I know you probably get this a lot, but I just have to ask..." Ann paused. "You are pretty short. So how do you manage to drive your vehicle?"

He laughed. "I knew that was coming," he replied stoically. "Well, I got two different ways."

He flashed two of his full-length fingers, which would normally appear like nubs to anybody else.

"Well, we leprechauns usually pull the car seat all the way up to the steering wheel and drive."

"Can you see over the dash?"

"Yes. I happen to manage that. So, if you see a car riding past you that doesn't look like anybody's actually driving, it's a great possibility that it could be me!"

Ann had a girly laugh that was so appealing. You couldn't tell if she was actually trying to be funny or just being a people person.

"Okay, so what's the other way that the lil' fellows drive." She had to ask.

"In one of my cars, I have this special built-in machine. It's hooked up to where the console used to be. You know, like between the drivers and passenger's seat?"

"How does it work?"

"The gas pedal and brakes are controlled by the movement of my hands. The steering wheel and everything else still work the same. It's just so that I don't have to use my feet. I can sit up on pillows to appear taller." He chuckled.

"Cool. I have actually seen those special machines in disabled folks' cars."

"Right! Me too." He winked then grabbed his bag, receipt, and change from Todd.

Ann and Todd watched incredulously as Tiny Tim walked out the door. They were quiet and motionless for several moments. Then, out of the blue, Ann inquired,

"Why do it always seem like all dwarves got big ol' booties?"

Todd smirked then let out a slight sneer.

"I don't know, but I was sort of thinking the same thing myself. It don't matter if they are male or female, every last one of them got big butts!"

Chapter 15

Captain Smith was sitting in his office, and, as usual, he was tapping his pen on the desk. "Here is the paperwork that you requested, sir!" Miranda chirped once she entered the office.

Captain Smith grabbed the papers that she handed over.

"You sure know exactly what to do and say to make me feel good as the boss."

"Yes, sir. I know my position, and I know how to play it well."

"That's actually why I ranked you right under me." He pointed his narrow finger at her.

"I'm a very optimistic person. If you look on the bright side of it, you are my only boss. Everybody else has to submit to me."

They laughed together because both of them knew she was telling the truth.

Smith fumbled throughout the documents inside the vanilla envelope. Even though he knew that all of the members on his team were proficient, he still double-checked things.

He was just programmed to adhere to the motto, "You can never be too sure of anything."

"I must say that curiosity got the best of me, boss."

"Mm-hmm." He looked up at her with that stern glare in his eyes.

"I have to ask. What was the rush to get these particular documents?"

"It has been brought to my attention that there is an outrageous number of rapes in this city."

He put his hand under his chin then suddenly rubbed his beard back and forth.

"The total in two months has surpassed the average for an entire year."

"I catch your drift."

"Of course you do! But my question to you is do you believe that this could possibly be the same guy every time?"

"There's a great probability. It's been reported several times that whoever they are wears a black mask. On several occasions, they had on the exact same pair of windbreaker pants. The crimes happened almost around the same time every time."

"Good work! I see you have already done your homework."

"Yes, I have. I've just been waiting on the go-ahead from you to apprehend the prick."

"I figured you would say that."

"Well, obviously you know me too well."

"However, during your analysis, you left out one important thing."

"And what may that be, sir? I thought that I covered a lot of ground."

"You didn't mention that these crimes happened around the same area every night."

"Pshhh!" Miranda blew out hot air. She couldn't stop pacing the floor. "How could I not catch on to that?"

He didn't answer. He wanted her to answer her own question.

"I know why. I get it." She bobbed her head in submission. "That's why you are my superior, and I am the underling."

He winked. "I want you to gather the crew and call a meeting early Monday morning."

"Okay." She stood straight up like a soldier in the army then saluted him. "I can't wait to catch this bastard!"

Chapter 16

W e called this meeting today because of the numerous rapes that have been going on in east Nashville," she announced in the open room. It was early, so everyone in the division had blank stares as they looked up at her. Most of them were thinking that this gathering was routine. They hadn't had their coffee, let alone their sweet cakes, so their brains weren't registering. All they did was yawn.

"I know this may seem routine, but it's not." It was like she was reading their minds. She then pulled out the wand that she used as a pointer. She directed the wand toward the board.

"In these particular areas, we have discovered that several rapes have occurred recently. As of now, we are not certain if there are several people doing these crimes or just one."

While their superior officer was giving her lecture, two agents in the far back whispered about how Sergeant Ross was google-eyeing the girls on the projector. He had always been weird to them, and most of Sergeant Ross's team figured that he might have been a rapist staged as a federal investigator.

"People!" She got louder to gain the whisperers'

attention. "Are you listening to me? I said that these crimes could very well involve only one man. That means a serial rapist is on the loose. Now, shouldn't that be enough information to make you people come alive in this dead room?" she yelled again.

The deputies were still off-track with her. Either they didn't appreciate the prominence of a woman or maybe she didn't have enough enthusiasm. Whatever the case may have been, all of them still seemed drowsy in the meeting. Captain Smith knew exactly what to do. He almost made commander in the army at one point. "If this guy is not captured, a lot of your jobs will be at stake here."

They immediately snapped out of the spell they were under. "Like your lieutenant was saying, something this serious has never happened right under our noses before. We will not tolerate being mocked in our own city. There must be compensation for crime. So, if criminals want to play then they must pay the piper."

The officers in the room were now lit with bursting energy. Ms. Thompson turned to smirk at Smith when hands raised from several members in the group. No one wanted to lose their job. So they began asking questions.

"Is there anything notorious about this prick?"

"Do we have the green light to shoot on sight?"

"Can you give us more information to go off of in the speedy capture of this person or these people?"

The captain felt irritated. "Whether convicts recognize it or not, studies have shown that repeat offenses often have the same patterns or sequences. Most of the predators don't realize it at the time, but it's always an advantage for us."

The team began pulling out their pads and taking notes.

"Their defaults help us track them down before they are able to strike again and again. Most times, they are not on high alert. They presume that no one is on their trail."

"What's the downside of the subject?" someone yelled from a far corner.

"The downside is that if they believe that they are about to get apprehended, the only option is death for them."

"People, we do not – I repeat – do not want another case to end like the Chad Rosenbeck case did." The lieutenant stepped in to take over the floor once again.

"Yeah! The rookie vomited all over himself at the sight," Agent blabbed, and the others laughed. "Agent Ross, we don't want to see what you ate from four days ago again."

There was an uproar in the room. Chairs moved, and bodies jokingly flopped around.

"Hey! Settle down, officers. This is a serious task that we have at hand."

The room was back under subjection as Captain Smith continued. "We all have had our fun, so take it easy on your colleagues and get some work done. Time is running out as we speak to bring this nightmare to an end."

The deputies said their goodbyes, gave their property, and then left. Only the two highest-ranked officers stayed. "Did you notice how Agent Ross spaced out peering at the ladies in the pictures?" she asked.

"Yeah, I did. You know I don't miss much. Do you think we ought to keep a closer eye on him or have his records rechecked?"

They looked at each other for a moment, laughed, then shook their doubts away. "Nah!" they both sang at the same time.

Chapter 17

You could hear both of them laughing and playing. Angie ran around in only her bra and panties, while Clyde chased her. He always refused, but for some reason this day, he finally wore the Tarzan outfit that she brought for him months before.

They had been into roleplay for years. They had already done everything from nurses, doctors, French maids, schoolgirls and lawyers. Now today they were Tarzan and Jane.

Clyde glided and caught his fiancée by the waist. In one swift motion, he picked her up then slammed her on the bed. She giggled as she bounced twice on the cushion.

"Me, Tarzan, angry at one-piece," he squawked in his caveman voice.

"Why, honey? Me, Jane, love it."

"Butt cheeks out and thong up my crack!"

"I like it, though, babe. It's cute." She pulled the string that made it snap back in place.

He raised up then began nibbling her earlobe. That was her spot. She couldn't resist sighing and squirming.

He rolled both of them over but moved her on top of him. They kissed gently like the white folks did for hours in the movies before they had sex – if they even had sex at all in the movies.

"I'm so glad you did this for me. It means so much because it has always been my fantasy."

"Anything for the queen."

"I've always wanted to see my man in a one-piece Tarzan outfit," she admitted while still sitting on top of him. "You know what? I owe you a huge favor for this."

"Yeah. I know it! And I will be collecting, too."

"Ooh, baby!" She reached down then hugged him tightly around his neck.

Angie and Clyde were inseparable. They had so much in common. They enjoyed the same foods, watched the same television shows, and they were both brunettes.

The two were so loud inside the house. They didn't recognize that the sound of their parade could be heard by anyone who was passing through.

The blinds were closed, but the window was up. Sadly, they didn't know that someone had been watching their episode since the beginning of the act.

"Psssh, babe. I have an idea. How about we try one of your fantasies also since you've been so good to me?"

"Two roleplays in one night." He held up both fingers. "Cool! We've never done that before."

"So, what do you have in mind?" she asked while looking directly into his eyes.

He was lying flat, so he lifted his body up against the rail of the bed to answer her question.

"I do actually have something in mind. But I don't want you to think that I'm creepy."

"Well…do you know the guy who has been on the news channel like every day?"

"Yeah! You mean the serial rapist or whatever they call him?"

"Bingo! That's him. The one they never caught."

"Oh. Okay."

"I want to pretend to be him for a night."

She giggled at him. "Why you want to be him?"

"I think it may be very interesting."

"It do sound exciting!"

"So, are you down with it?"

"Surely, if you could be my Tarzan, I can be your victim." She chucked loudly. "Okay, honey. I'm willing to participate."

"Wonderful!" He was so happy. "I'm going to get ready. I have to go in the garage and dig up my ski-mask and jogging pants." He immediately cut off the light switch then turned to leave.

The man who had been eavesdropping outside their house became curious. He tiptoed closer to the window, making sure that each step was taken lightly. He didn't want the sound of him stepping on the grass to become too loud.

By the time he made it to his destination, he peeped in and saw that Angie was tucked tightly under the covers. He wondered what she might be wearing underneath those sheets. Just the thought of her bare skin made his little man rise.

All kinds of images went through his brain. But first he had to make sure that his path wouldn't be blocked and his calculations would be on-point. At that very moment, a little more confidence flared up in him. He high-stepped around the side of the house until he reached the shed.

He put his ear to the garage door and heard Clyde on the inside rummaging through boxes and crates.

"Perfect!" he said to himself, after which he ran back to the other side of the house where he was in the first place.

He hopped in through the window and had half of his body dangling out. The noise immediately alerted Angie. She fell right into the role of her character. "Oh, my, Mr. Raper Man. Is that you climbing through the window?" She giggled.

The unknown man was startled. He looked at her, incredulous. While Angie tightly held down the blankets onto herself, the perpetrator wobbled onto the floor. It made a loud thump when his body hit the carpet.

"Who is that?" She chuckled. "Is that the man from Channel 13 News?"

He shook his head as he moved closer to her.

"I can't see you. But I can smell fresh cologne on you. Did you freshen up before you came to rape me, Mr. Raper Man?"

He shook his head again as he edged next to her. He stuck out his hand and rubbed it down her chest.

"No! I don't wanna," she said jokingly as she removed his hands.

He knew that time was running out before the real owner of the house came in, so he aggressively stuck out his hand and rubbed it down her chest again. She tried to move it out of the way, but his grip was too powerful for her. Angie liked the aggression of this man. She was instantly turned on. Never before had she been this wet in her life. Her hormones were raging, and her breathing was abnormal. She didn't know what had gotten into who she thought was Clyde. But she liked it. Truthfully, she always wanted to tell her boyfriend that he was too passive when it came to sex.

Playtime was over. The masked man got on top of his consensual victim, and then ripped her thong off of her body. To him, this was the easiest episode he ever had. As she squealed, he instantly grabbed one of her legs and cocked it into the air with his strong arm. He used her body as a crutch to stand up in mid-air as he slid down his pants, then Hanes. After that, he inserted his serpent into her hiding spot and went to work.

She mumbled as he went knee deep.

She was warm and tight. Only a few strokes had him nearly at his peak.

"Why you not saying anything?"

The man pumped but remained silent.

"Talk to me!" Angie demanded through stretched vocal cords. After moments of begging him to speak, she realized that he must have been enjoying himself too much. She was thinking, The cat must have his tongue.

Both of them began to sweat as minutes passed by. Who could resist the libido going on in the room? Body-to-body contact was the best sport or exercise that anyone could imagine.

She moaned as she bit down on her lips. She squirmed from side to side while working her hips into the action. "Clyde...baby...how did you get...get...so tiny?"

The man stopped in mid-stroke when he heard that comment. He looked at her in disbelief.

"Don't stop! Work that lil' pecker!" she screamed.

Just as Raper Man was about to finish what he started,

the bedroom door slung open. When the lights came on, it was like the whole world had stopped. Clyde could smell a strong odor in the air right before he ran and snatched the intruder off his fiancée. He began cussing like a sailor.

The masked man struggled to get up, but Clyde wrestled him to the ground. There were so many emotions in the house. You could have cut the tension in the air with a blade.

Angie didn't know what to do. The best sex of her life was with a man she didn't know.

The rapist maneuvered his way close to the window. As the duo exchanged blow for blow, all of a sudden, out of nowhere. All you heard was a loud crack.

The entire room was still once again. It was silent. The rapist man staggered from side to side. He reached for his forehead before he hit the floor.

Angie stood there butt-naked with the brass vase still in her hand.

"Oh, my god!" She placed her fingers over her mouth.

Clyde and Angie were hysterical. They didn't know what to do. Never had they ever been around a deceased person before, let alone killed anyone.

"Do you think he's dead?"

"I don't know," he replied. "But it did sound like dead-weight hitting the ground."

"What did we do?"

"We?" He immediately questioned her. "What, you speaking French now?"

Clyde wasn't about to take a murder rep for this broad. "It wasn't no 'we' when that man was digging all up in you. You must think I didn't hear y'all's conversation before I entered the room. I heard you talking about 'Don't stop. Work it, honey,'" he imitated sarcastically.

"Clyde, I can't believe you. Do you actually think that I would have the audacity to sneak a man into our house? And have sex with him after I knew you was supposed to be coming right back? Who do you think I am?"

She made plenty of sense to him. He had a dumbfounded expression on his face. "So, how do you explain what went on in here, then?"

"I thought that was you!"

Without any hesitation, the hoodlum jumped up off of the floor then hopped out of the window.

Clyde ran behind him, but by that time, he had struggled out of the window. The masked man had already pulled up his pants and made it halfway down the road. He didn't bother to chase the intruder. He returned to the house and alerted the authorities.

Chapter 18

It was a quiet day at the auto store. There wasn't much traffic going through the revolving doors. The radio was blasting through the speakers, and there was a sudden interruption on the local county station.

"This is a breaking news alert. The masked man has struck once again in the metro area. Another victim of rape has described the same villain that has been terrorizing others. This time, he entered a house with a male and female companion. The police have been alerted, and the only statement made by the chief is that he can't release any other information at this time."

"Wow!" Ann immediately said after the country music resumed. "This creep is really active."

"Are you scared?"

"No! I keep my mace and tasers with me at all times."

"I bet you got a box cutter somewhere in the big grocery bag that you call a purse, don't you?" Mark asked.

"I sure do," she happily answered. "I wonder why the spokesperson for the police department always saying that they don't have any additional information to dispense at the time?" Todd inquired.

"My guess is that they don't want the suspects to know that they are on to them."

"Or maybe they really don't have any valuable information. They may be as clueless as we are but trying to make it seem as if they are on to something."

"You may be right. It could be a scare tactic, huh?" Mark agreed.

"Mmhmm!"

"My cousin is an officer of the law…" Ann butted into their conversation. "…and he says that nowadays people make the law enforcement jobs easy. They don't have to do much because the world is full of snitches. Either somebody ends up telling on the criminal or they tell on their own selves."

"What type of person tells on their self?" Mark couldn't believe that.

"A fool!"

"I know that's right." Todd gestured. "They could have me on camera and show me perfect footage of myself, and I would still deny it was me." He laughed. "They will be like, 'Todd, are you sure this is not you? Because he got on the same clothes you have on now; he's your size, height, weight, and hair color…'" He laughed again. "I would still say, 'Nope, that's not me. There are many people in this world that are my size, height, weight and have my hair color. Besides…to a lot of people, all white folks look the same.'"

As the trio was having their fun, a strange-looking man walked in the store with his head down. He had on a dirty baseball cap, and his whole attire looked as if he been rolling around in motor oil all day. If one didn't know any better, they would say that he was a crackhead because of his abnormal movements.

They didn't pay him too much attention at first. They continued their frolicking until Ann noticed the man. Speed-walking towards the door with his hands, forearms, chest and shoulders full of stuff. He was toting so many items, they were tumbling over each other. They were trailing all the way down to his stomach and waist as he went down the aisle.

"Hey, sir!" she yelled, but the man didn't look her way. "You have to pay for those products this way!"

The man ran out the door. Ann rushed up behind him, but, after a quick sprint, she second-guessed the entire situation. There wasn't any sense in getting beaten up over what wasn't hers. She turned around and jetted to the phone. She quickly dialed 9-1-1 emergency.

Todd and Mark were in shock. They monitored each other's gestures and listened closely to the telephone conversation.

Subsequently, two young men entered the store giggling. "Bro, that guy just ran out of this store?" one asked while walking to the cash registers.

"I'm afraid so!" Todd answered sadly. The two guys were frantic as they heard the last words of Ann's phone call. She hung up the phone then screamed. "Oh my God. This has never happened before!"

She was in such a zone that she didn't notice the new customers until she double-looked. "Pssssh. Excuse my manners. I am so sorry for the inconvenience. How may I help you guys?"

"No problem. I didn't want to distract what was going on," one of the customers admitted. "I'm just here to buy an alternator for my '79 Chevy Camaro." He decided to diffuse some of the commotion with his wit. "You know how these alternators always goes out in the wintertime. It never fails."

"Yup," Todd added. "In the wintertime, it's batteries, starters and alternators that quit. In the summertime, it's always radiators, fan belts, gaskets and thermostats."

Mark went to the back of the store to obtain the item that the man wanted. After he rang their total up, they paid and left.

"The police still haven't arrived yet!" Ann was flustered.

"Yeah! You would have thought that they would have been hurrying since a white girl was the one who called," Mark joked.

"This is not the time to be funny, mister."

"Don't panic. They will be here shortly...or maybe later on."

"What do you mean 'later on'?"

"It all depends on which voice of yours that you used. If you used your black girl hip-hop voice, then they might not come at all. But if you used the signature Caucasian, then they may be here in the next few seconds." He laughed.

"Forget you, Mark." She folded her arms across each other. "Why you guys didn't help me, anyway? Y'all saw me running after that fool."

"I don't get paid enough to chase down thieves," Todd speedily replied.

"Ah. That's white folk stuff. Rarely do you see a black guy straying out of their job description. Besides, you don't know if these thugs have guns, knives or what. I'm not about to lose my life over a job that will have me replaced by the end of the week. Shoot. I want to grow old and have kids."

"I know that's right!" Todd agreed then slapped high-fives with him.

Chapter 19

Kreasha laced up her brand new pair of New Balance tennis shoes and began to stretch on the front steps of her dorm stoop. The sweat suit that she is wearing was so tight on her body that one would assume she didn't have on anything if it weren't for the coloring.

Given the fresh air and warmth of the night, Kreasha was getting ready for her daily jog. She was accepted into TSU as the first seed from her hometown in Tulsa, Oklahoma. Ever since she was a child, the greatest joy of her life was running. Now she had a full scholarship for track. As she put her feet to the pavement, she set the timer on her watch to make sure she got three miles in. She took off and strode sweetly, like her anatomy was music to the wind.

It was getting late, so a lot of the other students were inside. The guard waved at her when she passed the patrol stationary. She couldn't hear him because the earbuds in her ear played loudly, but she waved back anyway.

The stars in the sky were bright, and the moonlight was just right.

"I wonder if God names each individual star?" she asked herself, as she tried to count them to no avail.

Ten minutes into the jog, she had already begun to sweat. Knowing that a workout was useless if you didn't burn fat and calories by sweating, Kreasha understood that doctors said everyone should exercise for at least thirty minutes a day to stay healthy, especially in America, where obesity and diabetes were overwhelming.

She kept her watch close and breathed through her nose as she kept a steady pace. She jogged across Fisk University, down 9th street, then into the park. She was two miles from Tennessee State University.

Jogging didn't faze Kreasha at all. It would take more than an hour to get her tired. She practiced with her teammates during the day, but at night, for her own personal time, she decided to do extra just to be the best at what she did.

The park was quiet, and ducks waddled across the pawn. The breeze was feeling good, as she jogged past a man who was standing on the trail she was on. Unbeknownst to her, he began running next to her. About five seconds passed by before she felt the presence of somebody next to her. She glanced to her right and saw a frame but couldn't make the face out because it was dark, and there was close to no light in the area. She didn't want to panic, even though her heart had skipped a beat. Just to play it cool, she waved at him. He waved back and smiled like the grinch who stole Christmas. Before she could take off a couple more feet, he reached out and grabbed her arm sleeve. She immediately yanked away, but he was not in a mood to give up so easily. He intended to regain a firm grip on her but ended up empty-handed.

It was like grasping for air when he reached out because

she had sped up too quickly.

Kreasha never knew her full running capacity, but she was about to find out that day. A person may be able to run fifteen miles per hour on average, but when their adrenaline is pumping with fear, that fear adds five more miles to that fifteen.

However, on the other hand, when you are truly anxious to get something accomplished, your Superman extra strength and abilities kick in like the man running behind his victim.

Kreasha looked back at her aggressor and was surprised that he kept up this chase for her. In that day and time, not too many people were in shape. While she was engaging in this cat-and-mouse game, she used her free hand to hit the screen on her watch with one swipe of her finger, so it would switch from timer to a cellphone.

"9-1-1, how can I help you?" a woman asked so calmly through the earpiece of Kreasha's phone that she had been using just a few minutes earlier as a radio.

"Yes!" She breathed heavily. "I'm in Franklin Park near Jefferson Avenue. A man is chasing me, and I think he's trying to kill me."

"Okay, ma'am. I will send units to the area," the operator responded, while typing in her location on the computer. "They should be there shortly."

"Please hurry!" she yelled in fright.

When the unknown man heard his victim's conversation, he immediately assumed she somehow maneuvered to alert the authorities. With every ounce of vigor he had, he made a last attempt to snag her but couldn't. He stopped the pursuit and bent over with his hands on his knees. He was out of breath, hyperventilating, and vomited a few times. It felt like his lungs were about to collapse because he hadn't done that much activity since his high school days.

Kreasha was still panicking. She didn't realize that she was no longer the prey of this predator. She ran as fast as she could for three more minutes until she stumbled upon a patrol car. Exhausted but with relief, she sprinted to the vehicle and dove on top of it.

"What's the problem?" The Hispanic male officer asked her once he stepped out of the car.

Kreasha had to calm down to gather her words. Her breathing was hard, and her heart was still racing within her, as if it was about to jump out of her chest.

"The man..." She snorted. "He is chasing me." She pointed behind her without even looking.

The officer looked as far as he could see down the path but couldn't locate anyone. He assured her that she was safe with him. Then he pressed the button on his radio.

"Yes, this is badge 121483. I have arrived on the scene with the caller who made the pursuit complaint. The suspect is still at large. I repeat – the suspect is still at large. Have several units surround the park within a 30-meter radius. Pick up anyone who looks suspicious."

"Copy that!" the dispatcher radioed back before she alerted the other units to pick up any male suspect in the area.

Chapter 20

Agent Thompson barged into her superior's office. "Wake up!" she yelled excitedly and tapped his desk. "Hey! What's going on?" He asked in a dragging tone then wiped the crust from out of his eyes. "Is it moving already?"

"Looks like the big boss man had another long night?" she asked jokingly.

"Yeah! Wifey still got me in the doghouse."

"Um. You sure about that?"

"What do you mean?"

"Does she have you in the doghouse or got another man in y'all's house?"

The captain rose up in his chair. "Let's not have this discussion now!" he growled sternly. "This is not the place or time. And furthermore it is not appropriate for you to be questioning me about my personal affairs."

"Sorry!" She shrugged her shoulder. "I was concerned and wanted to bring something to your attention. I have known you and your wife for a very long time, and, naturally, I believe this shenanigan has been well overdue."

Captain Smith rubbed his face with his hand then let his hand down. "What did you originally come in here for?"

He sighed.

"Oh, yeah, that!" She snapped back to her feisty self. "We have a lead on the case we've been tracking. The local police detained a suspect last night after an attempt to cause bodily harm to a college student."

"Okay, that's a start. What are the charges that they are holding him on?"

"At the moment, they only have him for questioning. They have eight more hours of his designated 24 hours to be set free." She glanced at the watch on her wrist. "But you and I know as well as the police department there that this might just be the guy who has been raping all of these women."

Yes, this may well be our guy, but then again…I have been wrong before, he thought quietly to himself before he spoke again.

"What was the guy wearing?"

Miranda looked at the chart that she had legally obtained from the police department's system.

"Five-foot-seven. Caucasian. Black hair, blue eyes, wearing all dark clothing with a hoodie."

"Alright, then. Let's go get this mud duck and put him in federal custody instead of the state's. These state officers are amateurs. They may blow the case, and we may never be able to take this nightmare to trial."

"Let's ride!"

"Give me a sec to get myself together."

"No problem." She left the room.

After Smith brushed his teeth and washed his face in the bathroom, he had a quick wash-up then found Miranda so they could leave.

Within ten minutes of driving, they made it to the ninth precinct. When they stepped out of the car, they noticed that the parking lot was flooded with cars. It was clean and tidy on the outside as well as the inside.

They observed the nice-looking photos that hung upon the wall as they walked down the hallway. A few officers tried to stop them as they approached the chief's door, but Agent Thompson quickly flashed her FBI badge, forcing them to back away.

He knocked on the door, trying to peer through the window, but the blinds blocked a clear view.

A baldheaded black man answered the door. He was bulky-looking with muscles about to jump out of his neck.

"Can I help you guys?" he inquired then glanced around the department. He was actually wondering how anyone made it this far to his office without being stopped or at least warn him by phone first.

The lieutenant never put her ID away. She kept it cuffed in her hand and put it in the chief's face before she brushed past him, and Smith followed.

"What seems to be the problem?"

"Oh! So, it has to be a problem every time you see the FBI?" she asked, then flopped down in his chair with her feet propped up on his desk.

"You got some nerve coming in my office like you own the place." He walked over and pushed her feet off his desk. "Get out of my chair," he demanded with his thumb, gesturing the way that he wanted her to go.

She obeyed the order and nonchalantly stood at attention. Her militant mind caused her shoulders to square off and eyes to stare straight ahead.

"What brings you guys here?" He took over his chair, and, once he sat down, he felt back in charge.

"We have been doing an investigation on the notorious rapist in this area," Smith spoke up. "...and this department is stepping on our toes."

"It is plain ludicrous for you to say the state boys are stepping on your toes because apparently we're the ones who captured the guy."

"Rule number one: Never expect your suspect to be the actual perp," Smith stated. "This is America, where we are made to believe that everyone is innocent until proven guilty."

"You're right! Poor little ol' me," He chided sarcastically. "I'm sitting here talking like the guy is black or something. I'm acting as if he is already guilty until proven innocent. That rarely happens."

Lieutenant Thompson and Captain Smith looked at each other after the chief's statement.

"I know how the system is set up these days," the chief continued his ranting.

"Due process, correct?" she asked.

"No! It's all rubber stamped with me. The police, prosecutors and judges are all in one accord. Do what we have to do to get them locked up, and then do what's necessary to keep them there. If they are lucky enough to have a leprechaun or genie in a bottle, then they have a slight chance to give it back on appeal."

"Sir! With all due respect..." Captain Smith was in disbelief. "...I have no idea what you are talking about. Your brain just scattered for a moment there."

"We are federal agents. We are not with the good ol' boy

system you and your community have rigged." Miranda interjected. "We do our jobs the honest way."

"Then explain to me exactly why you came all the way downtown to my office." He was in a rage.

"We are here to take full control of the guy that your patrol picked up in the park last night," Smith informed him calmly.

"No, you're not! You feds expect us to do all the work, then you take credit for what we do as a unit. Y'all just sit around on your lazy, NCIC-picking bums then wait to claim something."

He was speaking angrily and popped his shirt collar to release some of the heat inside. "Well, I am here to tell you that won't happen on my watch." He spoke boldly then waved his hand, dismissing them. "So, you can leave now."

"Sir, this not a request, and we are not going to ask you gently anymore. You can release the guy to us or receive a citation from the government. It's your choice."

The chief of Nashville's ninth precinct thought to himself for a moment about what the two federal agents just told him. He knew the rules as related to chain of command. The only people higher than the FBI were in the secret service, and you might as well say the secret service is the FBI. He was in no position to tongue-wrestle any longer with the agents. He didn't get that far up in rank by being a fool. He stared boldly at the two agents before him as if he was attempting to pierce their souls with his eyes. He then looked down at his phone and pressed the speaker's call button. "Yes, this is Chief White, can you please have an officer come into my office to escort these nice investigators to the interrogation room?"

Chapter 21

Hey, you guys! Do you want to hear a joke?" the Hispanic asked. "Sure. Why not?" Todd and Mark looked at each other for a moment then slumped their shoulders. Ann hovered in the back to make sure that the guy didn't slide any item off the counter without purchasing it.

"Okay. You have to listen closely to get what I'm saying." He reached behind his back, grabbed his wallet, then pulled his credit card out.

"I was in my backyard the other day, then a policeman walked up on me and asked me why was I shooting all of these cans, so I turned around and told him that I didn't know it was illegal to shoot cans in America."

"Yeah. It's illegal to shoot cans or anything else if you are in the city limits, but if you go off to the woods or in the country, then you can just fire away," Mark advised.

The Hispanic man didn't respond. He just stood there with a strange grin on his face.

After moments passed by, Ann, Mark, and Todd stared at him. They were expecting some feedback, but he was still frozen with that spaced out look in his eyes and that troublemaker grin.

"What?" Todd finally reacted. "Was that the joke?"

"Man, if that was the joke, then that is the wackiest and dumbest joke I've ever heard," Mark added.

"See, you don't get it, amigo. I was shooting all kinds of cans. I was shooting Africans, Mexicans, Jamaicans, Puerto Ricans, and Republic Dominicans. But that was after I shot all the first cans."

"And what cans were those?" she asked with a smile on her face.

"Americans!" he screamed. They couldn't contain themselves any longer. All of them burst out laughing. It was like a roar of chuckling in the building.

"I must say that was pretty funny," Mark admitted while holding his stomach.

"Stupid but funny," Ann asserted.

"I know, right?" The Hispanic guy knew he would get a laugh out of them.

He handed his card over to the cashier. Todd rang up his total then packed his products in a bag. "You all have a great day!" he said excitingly before he grabbed his bag off the counter then turned to head out the door.

"That guy is hilarious," Ann said while looking at the fellow with oil on his pants, hands and shirt. "He is going somewhere. Maybe not to the top ten in comedy, but he's going somewhere."

"Yeah, he's going somewhere all right," Mark joked. "He's going to hell if he don't pray."

"Woo. That was the highlight of my day so far." Ann finally calmed down.

"Today has been a very slow day." Todd was slumped over with his elbow on the counter and his hand underneath his chin.

"Oh my gosh, Todd. Why'd you have to ruin the moment like that?" Mark inquired.

"Sorry to ruin y'all's escapade, but you know I'm telling the truth."

"Yeah, you are right, since I'm wasting the company's payroll money, so one of y'all clock out if you want to," Ann stated.

Before anyone else could react quickly enough, Todd rushed and took his work hat off and unbuttoned his shirt.

"Say no more. I'm gone." He dashed towards the door.

"Hold up, Todo." Mark amused himself. "You don't have to be in a rush to leave such fine company like us."

"Oh, my bad, I forgot my manners." He became sarcastic. "I didn't give you the option of leaving. Let me allow you the opportunity to leave before me." He motioned his hand towards the door.

"Nah. I'm good, bruh. I don't have anything else to do, so I might as well stay on the clock and get this money. You know what I'm talking 'bout?"

"Yeah. I know exactly what you talkin' about, brother. Get money, so you can make it rain on that new girl that you met at the expense of me. What's her name again?"

"Sherie."

"Oh yeah. Sherie! She is a mighty fine and thick situation. How are the both of you coming along, anyway?"

"We're okay."

"If you two had plans or something that has to be done then you know I will stay here and let you go."

"No, I'm all right, homie. Sherie has a counseling session tonight."

"Wow!" Ann interjected in their conversation. "So, you pulled a winner. That girl is a counselor. That is incredible."

"Yup!" Mark blushed. "She will be counseling a class for those women that the mad rapist has been raping around the city."

"I bet that is going to be quite touching." Todd sound sympathetic.

"I bet that she came up with that on her own. However, she did get the government to fund it."

"What's the name of her organization?" she asked enthusiastically.

"J. Kenkade, or you can log onto the website at J.Kenkade.com."

"I thought that was just a book publishing company that sells those interesting books and gives new authors a chance to get their material published without any hassle."

"It is!" he exclaimed excitingly. "But, at the same time, it is more than just a publishing company and book marketing agency. It is a movement. It's connected with Divas, a sisterhood, and also does life-coaching and work with people who have been abused, misled or confused in any area of their lives."

"Okay. I see. I must check that out, then."

"Cool," Todd said. "I will see you guys tomorrow. I'm about to make like a tree branch and split before our acting manager changes her mind."

They all laughed together.

"Yeah. You better hurry up and go because I don't have any problem with not saving this company any money."

Chapter 22

Within minutes, a deputy led the way for the two agents into the interrogation room. Once they were inside, they glanced around the cubby hole. The camera was conspicuous, and the room was as cold as ice. They stood against the wall and shivered for moments until the suspect was finally brought into the room. The suspect was handcuffed tightly and shackled down around his waist to his ankles. He had his head pinned down and was wearing the striped uniform that inmates usually wear. Lieutenant Thompson and Captain Smith could not get a good look at his face until he sat down and lifted his head up. When their eyes finally locked, they were hysterical.

"Agent Ross!" Lieutenant Thompson yelled. "Why are you being detained?"

"I was picked up last night and roughly handled by these patrolmen here."

"Why would they assume you were the suspect – this mad rapist man?" Captain Smith quickly inquired.

"Last night, I had decided to do some extra work because I am so determined to close this case that we have been scrutinizing. I noticed the similarities in the areas where the predator lurks. So, I took it upon myself to walk through the same neighborhood for hours."

"So, in other words, you were on a one-man stake-out without the rest of the unit?"

"Exactly!" Ross got excited. "I know I'm a rookie, so the majority of the bureau doesn't think much of me. I sort of...kind of..." He stuttered, as he waved his hand from side to side. "I-I-I wanted to crack the case by myself, so I could be like the celebrity of the bureau for a month or two. You know—" He raised the cuffs up with his hand while he pointed at his colleagues. "Something like you two guys. You two have mad respect and honor."

The chief wasn't sure whether she bought his story or not, but she had to play along to gather more information.

"In other words, you went out of your way to be a replica of someone else. Did you think you were going to win a medal for this or become employee of the month?"

"No way." He laughed like a nerd. "I don't want anything but to do my job. I love working for the feds. It's been my dream job since I was a child. Ever since I saw that movie with Martin Lawrence in it called 'Big Momma.'"

"I see." She folded her arms across each other then raised an eyebrow.

"Why didn't you tell this department that arrested you that you were an FBI agent?" The captain wanted to know.

"For one, they weren't going to believe me and would probably have mocked me. For two, I knew you guys would get the word and come down here like you are now."

"So, you're a wise guy, huh?"

"I learned from the best." Ross smiled.

"Right!" She turned her head towards the guard who brought him into the room. "Can you stay here with him while my partner and I converse outside?"

The guard immediately nodded his head indicating yes. He kept his serious look on his face for the whole discussion. On the inside, he was hoping he could have a shot at dating Ms. Thompson.

She motioned for her boss to step outside with her. After he followed, she whispered, "Do you believe him?"

"As of right now, we don't have a choice but to take his story into consideration. For Christ's sake, he is one of ours, Miranda."

"I know, but I don't trust anyone," she said and bit down on her lip. Anyone could tell she was speaking from her heart.

"You just don't trust him because he is weird and he has always given you the creeps."

"Well…you're right about that." She paced the floor back and forth. "He is an odd ball, a pain in the butt, and a sore thumb all put together." She giggled. "But he may not be a monster."

"Whether he is or not, I'm pretty sure that this department will swab his saliva with cotton balls. I assume he will submit to a DNA test. If he passes the test, then he is scott-free."

"And what about if he doesn't submit to taking a DNA test?"

"Then he still is scott-free. They don't have anything to hold him on longer than 72 hours. He is only being held for questioning.

"Well, you know how some of these criminals end up telling on themselves when law enforcement doesn't have anything on them?"

"Yeah, I believe their guilt gets to them or they end up calling themselves being smart and make up things that entrap them. Like, how can you be so smart but so dumb?"

"You're right. Do you want to get a cheeseburger, coffee, or something?"

"Yes, I am starving. But what about him?"

"Oh, he will be okay. We will see him in three days."

Chapter 23

Denise looked around the room and felt uncomfortable because she was the only black girl there. Well, the counselor was black, but that didn't count since she wasn't one of the rapist's victims. She continued to view her surroundings and noticed that the room was colorful with all happy colors – what society deemed happy, anyway. She sat on the edge of her seat alongside the Asian woman. They were in a circle so everyone including the counselor could see each other perfectly.

The counselor finally broke the silence. "Hi, everyone, my name is Sherie. I'm the life coach hosting this event. I know that we all don't know each other, but that is an advantage because we can open up to each other more easily. Most times it is hard sharing our true thoughts and emotions with people who we know will react a certain way, and sometimes we just don't want them to be hurt as well."

"Uh." Aleena raised her hand. "Who exactly are you referring to when you say 'we'?" she asked with a Spanglish mix. "Are you speaking French or what? Most advisors or life coaches such as yourself have never been through anything dramatic. You teach out of the books you read because you've never had a nightmare become reality."

"You shouldn't be so quick to judge people because you never know the ramifications or perplexing situations someone may have been through," Sherie said. "Have you ever thought of what may inspire someone such as myself to want to be a social worker or counselor?"

"No, I haven't." Aleena sat back in her chair and rolled her body.

Sherie monitored everyone's behavior. She knew that as a class with a lot of offensive and defensive women wasn't going to be easy. So she wanted to lighten the load by first speaking of herself.

"My life hasn't been all peachy and bright. I have gray areas from experiences as well. No one knows the true impact of what you've encountered, but it would be wise to allow the healing to begin. Keeping everything bottled up inside of you is like having a fresh wound but refusing to see a doctor about it or neglecting to put ointment or bandages over it. Pretty soon, that wound will get worse and uglier and perhaps cause other symptoms, which you may then be unable to fix or could even lead to death."

All the ladies in the room had different reactions to her statement. Each one of them wanted to open up because that was their reason for coming to the meeting in the first place. However, none of the ladies wanted to be the first to be candid. They all stared at the others in the room, hoping that the next person would take the honor of opening up.

"Well…I have a question." Leslie shivered with a pause in her voice. "How can not exposing our tragedies lead to death or unfixable things?"

"That's a good question," Sherie announced, then shuffled the notebooks in her hand. "The longer a trauma clings onto you, the harder it is to talk about it. Eventually you will never be able to rid yourself of it because it has sneaked in for too long, and you become comfortable with hiding and storing it inside you."

"But what about the death part?" another girl wanted to know.

"Not all deaths are direct, even though the majority are. You may become sick from worrying, depression, or anxiety. Perhaps you have memories, and the flashbacks cause you to run off the road and wreck. Or you could be cooking one day and become spaced out from the episodes and burn the house down." Sherie now noticed that she was getting the audience's attention. She enjoyed the warmth. "I have also seen third-party involvements. Victims no longer know how to react with loved ones or friends, so it ruins their relationships. They take their anger out on individuals who aren't aware of their emotional meltdowns, so the person harms them because they treat them in a way that is not respectful."

"So you're saying our actions toward others will cause an even more painful reaction?"

"Yes, resentment and contempt will build up in your spouses, friends, coworkers or family members because they don't understand why you are being so mean to them. Neglect, silence, revenge, and rejection also play a big part in this state of being."

"I don't want my loved ones to be pushed away from me," Angie declared. "I need them at this time."

"I don't want to push them away, either." All the rest of the women agreed. It was now an open floor.

"Exactly!" Sherie interjected. "Another point that I

would like to enlighten you about is that a lot of women feel ashamed, corrupted, or dirty because of what these animals have done. I am here to tell you that the shame is on the rapists. Once this guy is caught and prosecuted, then he will be the one embarrassed, and you will leap with victory."

"I have something that I want to share," Angie replied.

"Go ahead."

"I mean, this is a sharing class, right?" She looked around the room. "Right?"

The ladies didn't respond. They only nodded.

"I'm only going to tell you all this because I don't know you, and since I don't know you, I don't feel any commitment."

"Please do share," Sherie urged her on.

"The night I was raped, I cried and bathed for hours. I scrubbed my body inside out. I felt disgusted and devastated. I no longer wanted to be in my own body."

"I know exactly how you feel." Asa put her head down. "My spirit and sense of self were taken that night." Asa's eyes welled with tears as she continued to speak. "Even until today I've felt yucky."

It became silent in the room for several minutes, as each person seemed to relive their event. Sadness overtook the environment. Lack of closure was in the atmosphere. It was like everyone's bodies became debilitated at the same time.

"A sexual violation is one of the most grievous acts that can be committed. Eighty percent of the world's population don't realize the impact that it has on each and every individual."

"You are so right!" Leslie cried. "I don't know if I can ever trust any man again. I'm married, but I can't even stand my own husband putting his hands on me. I have flashbacks, and it feels so gross to even sleep in the bed with him."

"One thing that we must realize is that the people who have always been in our lives are not the predator. Similar male attributes may trigger an upset; when that happens, it is wise to snap back to reality." Sherie spoke in a soft, feminine voice. "But this also goes both ways. People have to talk to their spouses and significant others to help them understand what is going on inside their minds. Don't assume that they automatically know why you are aloof and secretive because doing that will mean they're unable to deal with all of the factors involving your circumstances."

"You make it sound easy." Leslie grinned, but her eyes were still watery.

"My plan is to walk with you through the dark tunnels of your situation so that you can see the light and live in a brighter way."

"A change of location would be nice. I have heard of other victims getting relief from burning their items, such as clothing, jewelry, purses or anything that relates back to the incident."

"That sounds enjoyable." Denise added her two cents in, then smirked.

"The main thing to remember is that you have to do whatever is best for you. If changing friends helps you recover, then so be it.

"It is so hard for me to look at some of my friends and relatives in their faces," one of the ladies mumbled. "I don't know what they think of me."

"Friends and family are there to be part of your support team. If they make you feel uncomfortable, then stay from around them, but for the most part, friends and family will be where your strength and courage come from. One shouldn't turn away compassion at times like this."

The building was once again clothed in silence. Each woman put her head down and began to meditate. Words are powerful, and the statement that Sherie made not only arrested their lingering thoughts but also began to circumvent them.

She knew that silence had a demanding yet compelling influence. Without saying anything, a person's heart and thoughts could be reached through invisible magnetic fields. Sherie allowed some more time to let everything that was being contemplated register in their minds. It was good to leave a session with a noteworthy impact. Any more consideration would only be overkill.

"Ladies, I am so glad you opened up tonight. Like I said before, this is the first part of healing. Know that there is a process to progress. Everyone may not be restored at the same time because it takes some of us longer than most. If we continue to stick together, then we all can make it through this. There is strength in numbers."

"Yeah. It's kind of like turning lemons to lemonade, right?" Aleena asked.

"Exactly! But know that in order to get the lemonade, one must stir and shake the product. So, with that being said, know that it's not going to be easy. Your brains will be rattled, but one day all the sourness will disappear. Sweetness will be your equivalent."

"I appreciate bonding with you girls," Denise lied.

"I'm glad the government got in contact with me so I could make it to this class. I'm not going to say that it's good that we had a bad experience, but I am thankful that I'm not alone." Angie looked to her right.

"How did you ladies hear about this meeting?"

"DHS."

"Facebook, Instagram, and Twitter."

"The government office called me, also," Denise responded after two other of the ladies in the room did. "I guess they're trying to make it seem like they are doing something to help us."

"Well...I hope you ladies come back." Sherie unfolded her legs, put her notebooks together, and then stood up. "Our classes will be every Wednesday and Friday. Please don't let any barrier get in the way of you returning.

"Okay!" they all said together. All the ladies rose up then hugged each other. They made a few nice comments about each other's hair, makeup, and clothes, then departed.

Chapter 24

Congratulations! We are gathered here today with the same objective–to snag a serpent," Smith explained. "I can't call him a cat because he is more than just a burglar. This creative perp slithers and slides. He is a treacherous and wretched person. He has poisoned our city with his venom, so he has to be captured and then caged or murdered."

"Guys, this is serious," Ms. Thompson added. "We have gotten calls from the military, government, and the president. All eyes and attention have been turned on us. The attention has been applied with pressure – everything is at stake."

"Okay. We are clear that we all have the same agenda here, sir…and, uh, ma'am. But my question is what do we do when we get a lead on the prints or just happen to see him?" one of the deputies asked.

"Do you mean as far as calling for backup or the amount of force you should carry out?"

"Both!"

Captain Smith cleared things up a little bit. "This is the most critical and infamous case that any of us will have.

Like the lieutenant was saying earlier, all is at stake here. We should always be meticulous no matter what. But at the same time, we cannot by any means let this criminal get away. If we have to damage someone's property or take someone's car to get the job done, then so be it. No cost is higher the price on this guy's head. And as far as the force to be used, his head is required to be on a platter if necessary. It's just a figure of speech. When you are doing your job, if two or three extra civilians have to be harmed so that ten or more can be untouched then do what you have to do. So be it!"

Agent Ross walked in right after that last statement was made. Everyone was impressed that he showed up with so much elegance, boldness, and confidence. He held his head up high and looked straight ahead and had his chest poked out.

"Glad you finally decided to show, sergeant." Captain announced with a smirk on his face.

"Glad to be here, cap." He said, abbreviating his title, and sat down. "Sorry for the delay, but I was late getting my hygiene together."

"You are excused. We were just about to go over the game plan for clamping down on the perp that you were falsely accused of being."

The room immediately went into an uproar. They giggled and cracked jokes about their coworker.

"Calm down, ladies and gents. I didn't say that for chuckles," Captain Smith assured them. "I was in a zone, and it came out the wrong way."

"Oh, it came out the right way!" another agent yelled.

"Okay. Enough with the funny guy stuff. We have to get

on the same page."

"Listen carefully, investigators—" Lieutenant Thompson interrupted the mockery. "This is the game plan that we have outlined thus far." She pulled out her pointer and directed it towards the bulletin board. "We have designated the areas of the criminal activities. To close in on the unknown suspect, we are going to form five separate teams. Each one of you will be in sets of two and come from every corner. The captain and I will begin in the center then come outward towards you. Does everyone understand or do you have any questions?"

"Yeah." A rookie agent raised her hand. "Let's get this correct. So, you are saying that one team will begin on Douglas Avenue, another on Guantin Road, one on Brooks, and so forth, and work our way up the center of the perimeter where we will meet?"

"Yes!" Thompson replied joyfully.

"So what exactly will you two will be doing?"

"Looking for suspicious movements. Anything that looks out of place or mysterious should be looked into. Go house to house and ask people questions."

"Okay. Gotcha." The rookie took down a few notes in her pad.

"Does anyone else have anything that needs to be cleared up?" She looked around the room for several seconds. After no one raised their hand or made any other type of movement. She gave her last words.

"Okay." She pointed to the center of the outline section. "It seems there's an auto store right in the middle of the area where the rapist has been doing these crimes. The captain and I will start at this location and work our way around to you."

"Now why an auto store is the location of the center point we have no idea." Smith stood up and spoke with a loud voice. "During my days of working for the FB, it has usually been a house in the center, but we have to do at times what doesn't seem right. I believe if we apply all our efforts then we will ultimately have a favorable outcome. As for now, you all are dismissed. Go snag a crook!"

Most of the agents gathered their belongings together then left the room. The only three left were the two highest ranking officers and Agent Ross. They all peered at each other in silence. They wandered what the next person was thinking.

"I have a question that I want to ask you guys, "Agent Ross said as he picked up his items off the desk. "When I was in jail, why didn't you take me out of there? I know you have the power and authority to do so."

"We knew they would release you on your own recognizance."

"How could you be so sure about that?"

"If you're innocent, then the justice system usually works."

"But you know like I know that the system has hiccups."

"Correct!" Smith replied. "Which is why I said usually works. Nine times out of ten, it's a buddy-buddy system of financial situations. The police may dislike that we take their cases when willing, but we are still their buddies."

"And another thing…if you had submitted to do a rape kit or mouth swab then that wouldn't have been a prob-lem," Thompson added.

"Yes! I gave them samples only because I saw the look

on your face. I am not guilty. I was only doing my job."

"Of course you were." Agent Ross shook his head then walked out of the room. Smith and Thompson stood back to monitor his movement.

"So, what do you think?" she asked.

"Let's assign a special agent to observe him. I think he is a 10-52, but no one can be too sure of anything nowadays."

"10-4 on that!"

Chapter 25

Hey!" he squawked then tried to squirm away from her tight grip around his neck. "Will you please let me make it into the door a little farther?"

"Oh. Okay." She stood upright to let him go. She observed him as he cleared the doorway. "I'm so sorry, but I say you're far off. I know that was you because your car is so obvious. I mean, with it being all yellow. I couldn't contain myself. I had to run and hug my BFF."

"I understand. How have things been going around the store?"

"Perfectly imperfect if imperfect is perfection." She smiled, which made him cringe.

"Huh?"

"Nothing." She shook her head. "Everything has been well."

"Good. I knew you could handle it."

"What's up, my main man?" Mark looked up from behind his cash register. He was servicing a customer. "I thought I heard your voice."

"Yup! It is me in the flesh." He walked over to Mark and gave him a handshake. "I'm feeling refreshed, man. It's like I've been rejuvenated or something."

"I can't say I know the feeling, but I will when it's vacation time for me. He smirked then handed the lady's remaining balance to her. "How long have you been gone? It's been, what, like maybe two weeks?"

"Not quite, but sort of. I took a few extra days than planned."

"The best thing is that you enjoyed yourself," Ann said.

"Yes, it sure is."

"So, are you back to stay or you want me to continue to be the boss? Because I sure don't mind being the boss lady around here. It sure feels good."

"No. I'm only here to see how the store has been running in my absence. I won't be coming in to work until tomorrow morning."

"So, where all did you go?" Mark wanted to know.

"Just to Paris, so I could cool off a bit."

"That's odd. I thought all flights were delayed because of the bombing attacks." Shane smirked. "Well, I guess I caught the 747 in the nick of time before all the delays."

"Oh. Okay."

"Tell us more, Shane," Ann sang. "Did you take any pictures? How about souvenirs? What was the most interesting part?"

"I went to see the Grand Canyon, and it was amazing."

"You mean the Eiffel Tower," Mark corrected him.

"Yes! The Grand Eiffel Tower, I mean." Shane wiped the sweat from his forehead. "Guys, I am really exhausted from my trip. I need to get some rest."

"Okay. You better make sure you show pictures of your experiences and destination at a convenient time."

"Alright. You know I will." Shane walked out the door

and just as he was leaving, a man and woman casually dressed brushed past him.

Moments later, Todd came wobbling out of the back corner of the store. He was looking tired as usual, but this time he was snacking on a bologna and cheese sandwich with a small bag of Funyun chips.

"Hey, Todd. You just miss your best friend in the whole wide world," Mark joked.

"And who might that be?" he asked with an expression on his face that was saying cut the games out.

"Shane McCarthy."

"Oh. I knew he was here." Todd took another bite of his sandwich then let out a huge and smelly burp. "That's what made me coming out of the parts department take so long. I'm not ready to see him, really. I don't know if I ever will be ready to see him."

"Man!" Mark waved the deadly fumes of Todd's burp away. "What have you been eating to have it smelling like a dead skunk coming up out of you?"

"Yeah." Ann fanned the fumes as well then ran a slight distance away. "It smells like that came from deep down within you."

"Too deep, if you ask me."

"I'm going to start calling you Big Burp. Yep, Big Burp is your name from now on." She smiled.

Todd's focus was shifted to two potential customers. They had been lingering around several aisles for a while. What caught his attention was that they were secretly watching everyone else.

"Hey guys. I don't mean to interrupt your dramatics, but have you noticed those two people looking at auto parts as if they are gazing at some random Walmart products?"

"Yeah. You mean the man and the lady who came in when Shane left?" Ann asked.

"I guess so," Todd replied.

Mark scanned the store with his piercing eyes to see whom they were referring to.

"Whatever their profession is, it must be elegant," she added.

"Yeah, right. Profession thieves."

"Awww. I see who you are talking about now." Mark finally located the targets. "The man and woman who are casually dressed?"

"Now he catches on." Todd sucked his teeth jokingly.

"Yeah. You are on the late show."

"Look how they are monitoring everyone in the store's movements, being sneaky and such."

Just as Todd finished his last statement, the suspicious guy peeped over the rack and noticed all of the cashiers staring at him. He put the display headlights down then got the attention of the woman beside him. They both looked straight ahead and walked to the front.

"Hi! I am Agent Thompson, and I work for the FBI," she said while flashing her badge. "We are currently investigating the numerous rapes that have been going on in our metro area." She stared at the three. "You guys wouldn't know anything about that, would you?"

To Ann, Mark and Todd, it seemed like they were just speaking a different language. They were in awe and didn't comprehend the words. Their train of thought was twisted after she flashed her badge with great authority.

Captain Smith stood back and didn't say anything.

He was more of the observer.

"Do any of you understand what I just asked?" She looked directly at Todd, and his jaw dropped along with his tongue hanging out like a thirsty dog.

"Uh…oh," he stuttered. "Can you please repeat the question, ma'am?"

"I said we are investigating criminal activities, specifically the numerous rapes that have been happening in our metro area. Would any of you three know anything about them?"

"Oh. Sorry." He shook his head to snap out of the trance. "It's just that I've never been around a real FBI. agent before."

"Yeah, it's like you came out of a movie and straight into our store," Mark added.

"I thought y'all always stayed hidden and confidential," Ann explained.

"Normally, we do. But today you have the great satisfaction of meeting two."

"I would assume that you guys are here for business and not personal reasons. Oh, what a remarkable occasion this is."

"Okay. All righty then, Mark," she indicated after his statement.

"What?" He was shocked. "How did you know my name?"

"It's right there on your work shirt!" She pointed.
"Oh," he responded with a dumbfounded look on his face. "Oops. My bad."

"Plus, we did a little homework on you guys before we got here."

"Just a little, huh?"

"Not much." She looked around with her captain still quietly by her side. "Where's your boss Shane?"

"Well...obviously you haven't done adequate homework." Ann shuffled her feet. She felt it was time to be straight up with people she thought were like ghosts to others.

"Shane took his vacation period so it wouldn't roll over to the next year. I don't know how you fancy people do it at that elegant building of yours, but if we don't take our vacation time here, then it's gone and we don't get paid for it."

"Have you ever read the gospels in the Bible?"

"Uh...what? Yeah of course," Ann stuttered. "But what in the world does reading Mark, Matthew, Luke and John have to do with Shane, Ann or you?"

"Well, let me explain it to you, Miss Lady." She put her hand on her hips then slanted her leg. "Jesus Christ asked people many questions. However, did you not think that he didn't know the answer already to the questions?"

Ann thought about what was just asked momentarily. She didn't reply. She only stuck her lips out and blinked because Agent Thompson was correct.

"Of course he knew the answers to the questions before he asked them to the people. Just like God knew the answer before he asked Satan where he had been in the book of Job. God also knew where Adam and Eve were before he inquired where they were."

"Okay. Point taken!"

"No. You don't get the point because I'm not through clarifying myself." Agent Thompson went on. "Sometimes people ask questions just to see what another person will say. That doesn't mean I was lost. Maybe I wanted to see who would lie so I could judge your character."

"I understand, sweetie," Todd was googly-eyeing the lieutenant up and down.

"I'm sure you do," she said with an attitude. "But I'm not talking to you, Todd. I'm talking to Little Miss Smarty Pants here."

"You know what!" Ann yelled. "I don't have to stand here and take this from you. Shoot, I don't even know you while you're coming all up in our store and acting like you running the place. You better calm down, heifer. I don't care who you are or where you work at."

"The thing about people like you is that if your brain were as smart as your beak, then you would be a genius."

"And the thing about people like you is that your nose is so far up your own behind, you have become immune to the bull crap." She waved her hand dismissively. "And I don't have to take this from you." Ann walked off angrily.

There was a duration of silence after that episode. Nobody else dared to move. It was like the entire atmosphere was stuck or the world was on pause.

Finally, when everyone was finished staring into space, Todd decided to make his move. "Listen, beautiful. I don't care what she says, but I think you are sexy when you're mad."

Lieutenant Thompson slightly smirked and shook her head at Todd's remark. "Ann just didn't know that she was seconds away from being charged with obstruction of justice and harboring a fugitive."

"Don't be so uptight. You just need a little loving, baby.

Perhaps a massage, foot rub or fix. When was the last time you were charmed or went out on a date?"

"Boy!" She flipped back to her serious side, but was still bubbly on the inside. "I am an official government worker. I don't have time for malarkey and gibberish. I am here for one reason and one reason only."

"So, you are so caught up in doing work for Uncle Sam that you can't enjoy your own life?"

"Yes!" She answered, then she pondered the response. "You are going to end up being one of those lonely old ladies who cuddle at night with a bunch of cats."

Mark giggled at the comment but stopped when he glanced up at Captain Smith. Smith hadn't said anything yet. He had a mean-mug look on his face the entire time.

"And the kittens will be your grandchildren," Todd continued to harass the woman.

"Here's my business card." Her speech slurred on the word "business".

"If any of you happens to see something suspicious or know of anything, then alert me. What you say will be kept strictly confidential."

"Okay." Todd gladly received the card." I will most certainly keep my eyes open carefully so I can have a reason to ring you." He held up his thumb and pinky finger to his ear as if it were a phone.

Captain Smith and Ms. Thompson turned to leave the store. They looked around at every detail of the building as they left.

Smith cranked the Buick up after the pair got in. He let the motor idle for a while then gripped his hands tightly on the steering wheel. He looked forward. Normally, when this happened, his mind was in the twilight zone or matrix.

"What's up?" Thompson buckled her seatbelt then crossed her legs. "I can sense when something is bothering you."

"I was just thinking…do you remember about the third or fourth rape that was reported?"

"Yes. The woman made a statement that she hit the intruder who came into her house with a vase. And the guy you were just talking to inside the auto store had a scar on his face that could be the result of that vase.

"You mean the one named Todd?"

"Yes."

"I'm afraid I saw that too. But we aren't sure if these crimes are actually related or if it's even the same guy involved in all of them."

"That may be true, but we are going to investigate them from every angle. I have a hunch telling me it's the same perpetrator, and I'm sure you do too." Captain Smith looked awkwardly at her again. "Don't tell me that you are getting soft on the case because someone was just hitting on you." He smiled. "Now, I know you haven't been charmed in a while, but we still have work to do."

She shook her head to snap out of the trance that she was in. "Uh…of course not," she stuttered. "I will never get soft on a case. This isn't the place or time."

"Okay, then. I'm just making sure. It's our job to keep one another on their toes." He winked his left eye then drove off slowly.

Chapter 26

Stalker man was at it again. He felt invincible, like nothing could stop him. He was a veteran at his profession…or, rather, his hobby. He knew that the authorities were all over the case, but in his mind, he was like the gingerbread man who couldn't be caught. He felt like taking his craft to a whole other level. Maybe he would begin kidnapping women and keeping them chained in his basement for days. He thought of what he would and wouldn't allow them to eat as he breezed through the night in search of another victim.

"Bread and water," he exclaimed to himself. "Yeah. Just like the old days. I will throw a few breadcrumbs and give them a drip of water to drink. Just enough to get the tip of their tongues wet. Yeah, that's what I will do." He rubbed his fingers together then let out a sinister laugh. "'Sex slaves' is what I will call them."

He was slightly going insane and didn't realize it. A supernatural force seemed to possess his inner being, and it flowed through his eyes.

He continued to prowl like a hungry lion in search of pleasurable flesh, wearing what he called his luckiest linens.

Every time he wore these particular black-on-black wind-breakers, he would score. He walked through the winding area about a mile from his house. He always took this route because it led to all four corners of the city limits.

This time he decided to travel down Brooks Avenue. Everybody knew that Brooks was the path that prostitutes and drug dealers coasted along. The police were cracking down on criminal activity in that area, but he figured that he would go undetected because he didn't look suspicious. He passed up several potential victims as the women made advances toward him, showing that they were ready and available. He wanted to be the one to choose his prey, not for them to choose him. So he ignored their seduction until he made it to Sands Motel. He spotted a specimen that truly interested him. She was standing alone under the deck of the building. Her jacket draped around her hips, and she had her hand against the wall with her purse slung across her arm. She must have heard his footsteps coming because she turned as he made it closer, and they made eye contact.

Lust was in the air from both sides of the perimeter. Neither could deny the locked google-eye.

She spoke first, waving her fingers. "Hi."

He gave her head nod from a distance. His stance indicated that he was interested.

"Why are you way over there? Come over here like you want to give me some of your good loving." She giggled. "I won't bite…unless you want me to."

He walked closer to her and looked at her up and down. He admired every inch of her five-foot-eleven frame.

"So, I guess this is what the hood calls thick?" He giggled.

"You can call me what you want as long as you got a grip." She then took in his physique. "Hmmm!" she purred. "I know your money better be right."

"Of course," he said with authority then walked off. She followed behind him.

He led her to a trail behind the motel. He didn't really know where he was going, but he knew it was dark and secluded in the direction where he was heading.

After five minutes of trailing and silence, the prostitute spoke up.

"Where are you taking me?" she asked. "Don't you think we came far enough to do what we have to do?" She looked around the creepy area. It was actually a rocky road with grass and weeds surrounding it that hadn't been cut in ages. "We can stop right here and let you get a quickie," she purred again. "I know you ain't nothing but a one-minute man."

She placed one of her fingers into her mouth and sucked on it. He reached out and grabbed her by the throat. His strong arms squeezed her voice box, Adam's apple, and esophagus. For a moment, she couldn't breathe. She struggled to remove his grip from around her neck while simultaneously gasping for air. Everything was going his way. In his mind, he had the situation under control, so he decided to advance. He kept a tight grip clasped onto her with his right hand then with the other hand, he ripped her shirt and bra off.

Out of nowhere, she gathered some kind of supernatural strength, balled her fist up and let loose on him. She swung like Layla Ali on the fool. She must have had some haymakers or one-hitter-quitters because he staggered and almost fell. His knees hit the ground, but he balanced himself with his fingers to avoid a knockout. She bounced back like she was doing the Ali shuffle. The situation quickly went from the norm to strange to undecided.

"You call yourself trying to take something, sucker?" She waited for him to stand completely up then began to peck on him again.

Bink. Bink. Bink. She unleashed a series of combinations.

For the first time, Mr. Stalker Man noticed how huge her hands were. He was seeing quadruple, and colors were changing to 3-D. For a moment, he rushed her and snagged a hold of her. They wrestled, and her breast smacked him in the face. It must have gone into his mouth because he frowned and spit like something salty was on his tongue.

She broke loose, backed up then held her dukes up. "Oh. You must not have known." She danced around him with her dukes still up. "I got them hands, don't I?" She reached out and stole on him again. He swung back like he was a prissy white girl. "Some call me Ricky, but others call me Nicky. Do you get what I'm saying?" She swung at him again, but this time he ducked the punch. "I try to be so lady-like at times, but it's dudes like you who make the man come up out of me!" Her voice became very deep.

A switch clicked on in his head. "You are a transgender!" he cried out.

"Yup! Sure is." She picked up her purse, shirt, and bra from off the ground. "Nice boob job, huh?" She gripped a hold onto her cleavage. "And I paid a pretty penny to get it wacked off downtown and had it surgically removed, so I'm all girl now."

"Oh my gosh!" He full-on kneed and screamed with

both hands on his face. "No!"

"Yeah!" She walked up on him then slapped him as hard as she could in the face. "So, don't you go barking up the wrong tree again. Desperate man out here trying to rape us and such." She rolled her eyes, snapped her neck and shoulders, then pranced off. When she got around fifteen feet away from him, she yelled out, "Oh! And I'm telling all the girls to be on alert for you, so they won't become victims of circumstance. Plus, I'm telling them how you got served! And just in case you don't know my name, it's Ricky Minaj."

Chapter 27

Another meeting was taking place. As usual, the attendants were dragging, taking their time to enter the building. However, most of them arrived in the parking lot at the same time. One lady pulled the last drag off her cigarettes, while others contemplated whether they should go inside or not. It was a decision that could determine the outcome of their lives, so they concluded it would be best to go through the entrance. Besides…what else did they have to lose?

Once everyone was gathered inside, they participated in small-talk while drinking coffee and eating the cheesecake that Sherie had brought for them.

Sherie meticulously observed her clients. The sweets and caffeine were a trigger to expose their innermost thoughts, but no one expected that from their psychologist. The ladies assumed that it was an innocent gift. They never figured the treatment would make them hyped as well as talkative. This is why people must glance beyond shenanigans at hand, especially when something is free.

She cleared her throat. "Excuse me, ladies." She motioned with her fingers for them to come. "Can I have your attention please? Class is about to begin, and you all know how limited our valuable time is." Sherie was the type of person that not too many people could refuse. She was charismatic, sweet, and soft-spoken. The ladies immediately flocked around her and took their seats. "Today, I want to continue our conversation on healing because healing and closure are what all this is about."

Just as Sherie finished making her statement, the doors to the building opened, and an unknown woman entered. She walked with straight posture and was built athletic, young, and certain of herself.

"Hi, ladies! I hope I'm not intruding, but the rape crisis hotline gave me this address. I was nearly attacked the other day, and I feel the need to be around comfort."

"Okay, sure thing." Sherie quickly rose to her feet. "Just grab a chair from that corner over there and bring it to our love circle," she directed.

The young lady did exactly as she was told. Asa, Aleena, and the rest of the women scooted over to accept her in the circle. Denise now felt more comfortable because she wasn't the only black attendee in the room. The rest of the women were either Asian, Hispanic, or white.

"Oh. And, by the way, my name is Kreasha. "She touched her breast when taking the privilege to introduce herself.

"Hello, Kreasha," all the women sang together.

"Hey." She crossed her legs.

"Welcome to our love circle, Miss Kreasha. I suppose you already know our days and time of visitation because you are here."

"Yes!"

"I don't have much to catch you up on then since we are just beginning. Um—" Sherie flipped through her notepad. "—I was just about to go over the recovery process, but something draws a reference to what you stated. What exactly do you mean by you were nearly attacked?"

"I was leaving from school one night and was pursued by a man that I believe was trying to rape me. I have been hearing about this guy on the news, and I believe in my heart for some reason that this is the same guy who assaulted you all and tried to get me."

"So, you wasn't actually raped?"

"No, so forgive me if I shouldn't be here."

"Awww," The group said. They each went over to hug her and show support. Some shed tears.

"You belong here, my darling. You have been traumatized at such a young age and need recovery like the rest of us. If not, you will develop long-term PTSD."

"What's PTSD?" Asa asked.

"It's post-traumatic stress disorder. It causes nightmares, tension, and illusions when you are awake."

Denise motioned like she was about to puke. Her head wavered back and forth. She covered her mouth then got up and ran.

This happened out of the blue, so the rest of the ladies were lost in thought. They didn't know if it was something that was said, done or one of those illusions that Sherie had been mentioning. After the counselor stood to chase her, the entourage followed. When they made it to the restroom, Denise was on her knees and bent over the toilet. She was vomiting repeatedly, so Sherie came up gasping for air then went back to plant her face above the toilet seat.

"Oh, my god!" Angie proclaimed. She was stunned yet sympathized. "Should I call the ambulance or someone else?" She staggered, contemplating whether she should leave the room or not.

"No, don't worry about!" Denise gestured with her hands. She turned to face her surroundings then turned back to get the last of throw up out. She wiped her mouth and jaw with the back of her hand.

All the women gathered around Denise to lift her up. It was a struggle at first, but the mission was accomplished. They led her to the sink where she washed then rinsed her hands and mouth off. She giggled at the steaming hot water.

"I don't have any Listerine or mouth wash, but you can have some gum." Leslie dug in her pocket and offered her a piece.

Denise willingly accepted the gum then pulled herself together. "I thank you ladies so much. I see that all of you are so caring, concerned, and compassionate."

"What is the matter?" Sherie asked.

"I have been very, very, very lightheaded and nauseated lately. And the reason why I told her not to call the ambulance is because I have already been to the doctor." She wiped her mouth in an attempt to dry it.

"So, what did the doctor say?" Aleena asked in her soothing Spanish accent.

"I'm pregnant."

"Awwwww!" The ladies gave her a group hug, all wondering who the baby's dad was. Denise cried. It was now a highly emotional atmosphere. "I'm six weeks pregnant by the guy who…who raped me."

Just when she thought that the group hug couldn't get any tighter, it did. All kinds of thoughts lingered in every single individual mind.

Chapter 28

I'm just going to be honest with y'all. I'm not going to front or anything like that. I don't have any leads," one agent announced after he threw both arms up in the air. "I know that this a progress meeting," another said, admitting, "But my mission's been blank likewise."

"Well, I'm checking on a few people who came under my group's radar," Sergeant Ross said. "We are investigating people who have been involved in past sex crimes."

"Hold up! Does that mean that you will be checking yourself out then?" A third officer joked then everyone in the room laughed.

"I'm not going to stoop down to your level today. I'm going to be a bigger and better man by keeping it professional." Ross turned to face his critics with an undermining glare. "It takes more to remain humble than it does to make an incorrigible statement, you know?"

The room was suddenly quiet for a moment while everyone tried to figure out what on Earth Ross was referring to. After a split second, they concluded that everything was not meant to be understood.

"If you try to understand everything a crazy person does then you will wind up being crazy yourself!"

"Is there anyone else whose positioning point isn't empty

or compromised?" the captain inquired.

The crews looked around stoically at each other, hoping that one of the others would speak up. They didn't want to make it seem like they weren't working to make progress. Plus, they didn't want to bring heat onto themselves. Sometimes, a person can work harder than they ever had before, but if nothing is there, then they cannot turn it into something.

"I see!" He stood up with his mean mug. "You must put more pep in your step. Sleep will not pay you like your job, so make something happen. Do magic, dig in dumpsters, crawl under rocks or bend over backwards for Christ's sake. It's been over a week."

They all looked dead now.

Captain Smith was furious. If one had a creative imagination then they might envision horns growing out the sides of his temples. The expression on his face indicated he was trying to give an explanation to idiots. "So, why are all of you still sitting there?!" he screamed. "Go, do some investigating!" He waved both of his arms in a gesture of dismissing them.

The teams immediately rushed out of the room. They moved so swiftly that a few of them bumped into each other. No one was in the mood to lose their jobs that day. They felt the quicker that they got out of sight, the sooner they would leave his mind.

After the squad left, Smith looked at Thompson and said, "I got something that I want to show you." He walked off, and she reluctantly followed.

Once they made it to his office, he immediately took a seat then pulled out the files that his secretary had brought to him before. When they threw them up on the table, the papers and sealed folders made a loud thump.

"Have you considered running a background check on the auto store workers?" he asked her politely.

"Uh. Actually, no, I haven't. I was going to give it another week or so then do a follow-up there."

"The reason why I asked you..." He scratched his head then finished his statement. "I asked because I couldn't get them off my mind. For some reason, I constantly get an awkward feeling at the thought of them." He opened the files then scanned the page while his lieutenant hovered over his shoulder to get a peek. "The only black guy who works there is Mark Price, and he has worked there two years less than Shane McCarthy. Shane is the manager and has been there for eight years. They are all friends with your admirer Todd Murray. The three of them have been long-term friends and graduated from high school together."

"Okayyyy!" She said, dragging the word out.

"Hold up. Wait. I know you think that they will all check out to be 10-52, but give me a minute. I'm going somewhere with this."

Miranda turned sideways then placed her hand on her hip.

"Mark and Shane both grew up in nice homes and don't have any criminal records, so they checked out, but Todd grew up in a drug-abusing household. His mom and dad fought often, and he has criminal mischief misdemeanor charges."

Her eyes bulged.

"There's more." He pointed a finger for her to pay careful

attention. "The lady you had your confrontation with is Ann Rodgers, who was originally born Andy Brandon Rodgers." He smiled. "So your baby girl is a boy!"

"Never in my years of working have I heard such a thing. Oh my God!" She put her hand over her mouth then paced the floor. "She had me fooled! I can't believe this."

"I can. In this field of work, I have learned to take nothing for granted, expect the unexpected, and never, ever under any circumstances be surprised."

"But look how long you have been working for the bureau. What, maybe twenty-five or twenty-six years?"

"Twenty-eight," he proudly answered.

"I only have fifteen."

"That's okay. Just keep living, and you will learn a lot."

"I take it we have more visiting to do?"

"Well, of course. I have to talk to your boyfriend Todd Murray and little Miss Andy Rogers."

She smirked.

Chapter 29

W e are going to do something different today. Instead of talking about healing and recovery, we will be focusing on prevention and safety." The women in the circle acknowledged the counselor's advice and welcomed the shift from their previous conversation.

"Does anyone here know of any ways to prevent attacks before they happen?" Sherie asked.

"Yes!" Aleena's hand immediately went up. "Purchase a gun?"

"A knife," Asa added.

"Mace, pepper spray, or a switchblade," someone else yelled out.

Sherie's face was filled with contentment. She knew how women in their predicament could easily be persuaded to turn to violence. She understood that weapons were a source of protection, but it could also cause more trouble. "Okay. Those are means of definite defense, but what if you didn't have access to those guns, knives, and pepper spray?" she inquired. "Take it from me, for instance, I don't own a weapon. I may have a few dull knives in my kitchen, but other than that, I don't have anything that will harm humans." "I believe in securing myself, so nothing like this will ever happen to me again. I don't have a gun, but I have started taking karate classes," Leslie admitted.

"Now, that's a start. I understand that you have been hurt, so you are willing to do whatever it takes to be safe. But we still should not let our circumstances make us completely bitter. Please remember that soft and sweet lady still deep down inside you." Sherie pointed at each one of them individually. "Bring it down a notch."

"So, what would you suggest?"

"I would say that it's the little things that count like making sure your windows and doors are always locked at your home and inside your cars."

Asa raised her hand, "Ooh. I live alone, so I brought a starter for my car that starts with click of a button. So, I don't have to go inside until my car is already started and ready to go."

"Nice," Angie declared. "I need to get me one of those."

"I have heard of motion sensors and lights outside of your house, so if someone is snooping around then lights will shine on them."

"We can also try to never be alone. Always make sure two or three other people are with us, I suppose."

"Yes! These are all excellent choices. It is wise to have somebody with us when we go places or handle business during the day."

"But these are our lives. We should be able to live them how we want to," Kreasha cried. "We shouldn't have to go through all of these changes for the next person."

"It's sad, but it's true that we shouldn't have to change our patterns and living conditions for others, but if we want to minimize crimes, then this is something that we must consider. The earth doesn't always coincide with our thoughts?"

"You are right. These are things that we should be aware of." Denise took control of the conversation. "There are a lot of peculiar things that we don't have knowledge of. I was watching TV the other day and saw how hackers hack into our homes through baby monitors, computers, and other electronic devices."

"Wow! That is insane. So, they've tapped into baby monitors and can hear when we are asleep or at home."

"More than that, they can hear every plan that we come up with. It's like they are taking a sneak peek into our lives."

"Now that's cold-blooded." One of the ladies shook her head in disbelief.

"I really appreciate these meetings," Kreasha admitted. "I am learning so much. And I feel close with you all. Hopefully, we can become good friends with each other if you ladies choose to."

"Oh. Absolutely."

"I already feel like I've known you all for a very long time."

"Exactly! Like we are sisters from another mother or something."

They all smiled at each other.

"I feel we are making progress and reconnecting with our inner selves. I am proud of every individual," Sherie announced. "And, with that being said, this concludes our session for today. Make sure all of you come back next week."

"Thank you for taking the time out to treat us."

"You are welcome."

They all stood to hug each other then departed.

Chapter 30

It was a busy day at the Auto Zone store. This was typical since it was the first of the month. The double doors were opening and closing repeatedly with too many customers to keep count of.

The team of four was all present, working hard, and sweating. Shane had to constantly empty the cash registers out because the overflow of money. Todd was in the back of the store getting out oversized parts, while Ann was in the aisle stocking the shelves. Captain Smith and Agent Thompson went in the building unnoticed and walked directly up to Mark while he was accepting a payment from an elderly lady.

"Hi. How are you doing, Mr. Price?" Captain Smith spoke first.

He peeked up to see who was calling his last name like that. To his surprise, it was the same FBI agent from the other day. "Hey! You guys are back," he said, then signaled for Shane to come over.

Smith continued his conversation once Shane arrived. "Mr. McCarthy. I was just speaking to your coworker. I don't know if you are aware of who we are or not. But I work with the bureau." He flashed his badge.

"Yes. I'm very aware." His eyes popped as wide as a mosquito. One would have thought they discovered blocks of gold. "My team mentioned that you were here a week and a half ago."

"Yes, we are here on unfinished business."

"To do a follow-up," Thompson added.

"Okay. Speak your peace."

"We have checked your workers out, and you two are not on our radar. However, I would like to investigate—" He thought to himself for a moment. "—no, excuse me. I would like to interrogate Todd Murray and Ann Rogers."

"I have no problem with that. Although I don't have the slightest idea why you would want to interrogate Ann. On the other hand, Todd has been acting suspicious for some time now," Shane snitched. "I am on the borderline of firing him. He is always sluggish and not alert and comes into work late."

Todd walked up and stumbled right as Shane finished his sentence. He was nervous to come out from the back of the store.

"We were just talking about you, Mr. Murray."

"For real?" Smith replied. "Of course, we are for real. So, you can either answer the questions that we have to ask you here or we can take a trip to the department downtown."

"Uh. Okay." He stuttered. "I have nothing to hide. You can ask me whatever you like."

"Okay, then. Where were you on June the ninth, July the first, July twenty-third, and last week?"

"I don't remember." He had a dumbfounded expression now. "It's not like I keep journals of where I've been. It's not like I wake up every morning and say, 'Today I will keep track of you every moment and remember day by day where I am."

"You're a wise guy, huh?"

Todd shrugged his shoulders.

"Can you explain that mark that you have on your chin? If you are our rapist suspect, then we want to know because during the crime, the woman hit you with a vase, right?"

He rubbed the side of his face. "I have no idea what you are referring to. I got this tiny scar from my other job at the factory."

"What other job?" Ms. Thompson asked then examined her books because he didn't thoroughly check Todd's background.

"I work at a factory on the south side called Cenveo. We stock newspapers, and I was driving the forklift when a stack fell from up high and scraped me."

Smith hummed. "So, if we ask Cenveo about this, will they verify what happened?"

"Yes. They have no choice. The accident could have been worse. Luckily, I jumped out the way in time to avoid a stronger collision," Todd explained. "Cenveo tried to give me some days off work, but I refused because I needed the money."

"Okay. We will check into that. So, tell me why you have been getting complaints about coming in all sluggish, tired, and without good work performance?"

"It's because I'm just so tired. I work the night shift at Cenveo, then come straight here." He glanced over at Shane with a mean mug on his face. "And also the reason why I've been coming in late is because of the traffic jams on the highway."

Shane and Mark couldn't believe their eyes. Todd never told them about his other job. Now they understood his poor performance. They would now have to make up with their friend and work around his schedule.

The captain jotted some writing down in his pad. "I have no further questions. We may or may not get back with you. We will just have to see." He turned to search the aisle for Ann. Miranda trailed him until they located her. "Andy Rodgers," he called out.

She was on the floor with a pile of items near her. When she heard her government name, she was stunned. She looked up with those beady eyes of hers to see who was calling her. Then she raised up slowly. "So what? You figured me out. Whoopty whoop! Is it a crime to have my name and sex changed?" Her neck was popping and rolling.

"The best thing would be for you to calm down, sir... ma'am...or whatever you choose to specify your gender as." The lieutenant couldn't hold her peace.

Andy batted his eyes.

"We are doing a thorough investigation on the string of crimes in Nashville."

"I'm aware of that!"

Neither of the agents said anything further. They had a stand-off with her to allow her to check herself.

"Oh my gosh!" Ann ran from side to side, then put her hands in her face and gawked. "I can't believe this. You guys cannot really think I'm the guy who's been doing these heinous things."

They remained silent.

"I'm transgender." She now stared into their eyes as if she

were searching for their souls. "You guys even know what that means?" she yelled. A few customers on the aisle with them were frightened off. Next, she decided that her words were not convincing to these uppity officers. "I had my manhood whacked off long ago."

The agents didn't budge.

"I take it that you two don't believe me, then." She was hysterical. "I will show you, then, and make believers out of you." She began unbuckling her pants. By that time, her pants had dropped to the floor. She raised up her shirt to reveal her clean-shaved split. She even took it upon herself to spread her legs even wider.

The investigators couldn't move their locked eyes. They were all the way zoomed in and wondered what doctor might have done the surgery on her. Before Ann could pull up her pants back up, an elderly white Man walked by with his six-year-old grandchild on the aisle. He immediately covered the kid's eyes after they got a view of her bare butt. He backed the child and himself away slowly then went to the front of the store.

"Now you see that there is no way that I can rape anyone if I don't have a penis. That Johnson was whacked off long ago!" Ann screamed and didn't care who heard or saw her since she was now out of the closet. "So, the next time y'all come barking up the wrong tree, please make sure you have all of your facts straight!"

Chapter 31

W e will be trying something different again today," Sherie announced. "Instead of conversing about healing, recovery, protection or safety, we will be on the subject of beauty."

"Okay." The ladies got excited. They all sat on the edges of their chairs.

Sherie smiled. "I knew that would get your attention. All ladies want to feel sexy and beautiful. Even the Bible declares that we are fearfully and wonderfully made. We are a royal priesthood."

"I know that's right!" Kreasha rolled her neck then crossed her legs.

"This class is about advancing. We will not stay in the mud. It is to uplift our spirits as well. We have to talk about the bad experiences to in order to face it but once we face it, we can bury it." Sherie enlightened the crowd. "So, who wants to go first? Who wants to talk about what makes them feel beautiful?"

Leslie's hand went up first. "I like when I get cute compliments."

"Attention is what makes me feel inspired and makes me smile."

"Oh, yes. Like when I'm in the grocery store or at the

mall, and a random guy compliments my nicely-shaped booty, toes, or breasts."

"I love people mentioning my gorgeous smile, eyes, or face."

Each one of them had a chance to say what delighted them. They were all giddy and feeling like schoolgirls.

"But hold up! Wait a minute." Kreasha stopped the fun. "Aren't most of you ladies married or have a boyfriend?"

"Girl!" Leslie waved her hand. "We didn't say we react or engage in the comments. We just like some extra attention that doesn't always come from home."

"I know that's right!" They all laughed and slapped high-fives together.

"Oh. Okay." Kreasha nodded her head. She was happy to be game tapping. "Well, I like to get my hair and nails done because that's what make me feel special."

"Yes! Yes! Yes!"

"What about going to a body spa to get a full body massage?"

"Indeed. I must get these knots rubbed out from under my skin. Plus, my bones be all settled."

"Who knows what else will make us feel all womanly?" "Have y'all heard about this company called Necessities in Australia? It's owned by a beautiful woman named Vanessa Fedora," Angie said.

"I think I have. She's the one that you can contact on Face-book, right?"

"Yup. Just go to her page called Vanessa Ferris or to her company called Necessities. She's on Instagram also."

"What's her brand all about?"

"She teaches people about what they are putting on their

skin and how everyday products are doing most people harm than good," Angie said.

"So, you mean her brand is about caring for the environment, too, but she's also passionate about educating those who are not aware that most products they use cause skin allergies, cancers, behavioral changes and a lot of other problems which people tend to cover up with the use of medication?" Leslie guessed.

"Wow! I didn't know that the products we use on the outside of our body can cause mood swings and behavioral problems." Denise was intrigued.

"We learn something new every day," Sherie informed.

"Sure do. I can second that." Aleena crossed her legs. "Tell me more about Necessities."

"Well, there are fourteen different soaps, each serving a particular purpose. Lavender is for calming and relaxing, ylang-ylang is for romance, mandarin for uplifting your spirit, and so forth."

"Do they scrub that exfoliate off the skin or have all essential oil and natural ingredients in them?" one of the ladies asked.

"Yes, the skincare has clay that removes toxins in the body – the brown and white clays exfoliate and leave the skin soft. There are moisturizers and eye creams that take away the puffs."

"Do they have a choice to buy wholesale?"

"Of course, and everything is for reasonable price."

"So that's how you keep your skin and hair so silky and clean?" Leslie rubbed Angie's smooth structure. "It's how you look so young and beautiful?"

She smiled and blushed at the same time. "I used to have

acne and dry skin. I couldn't find a cure until I ran across the Necessities website. I never knew that a healing would come way from Australia."

They laughed together. Sherie loved when women bonded together. She didn't mind them having girly talks. "I'm going to definitely check out Vanessa Fedora's Insta-gram and Facebook pages."

Chapter 32

W hy do you think those detectives wanted to talk to Ann and Todd the other day?" Mark asked after he finished sacking up a customer's products. "You mean those FBI agents?" Shane humped his shoulders. "Man, I have no idea. Maybe they believe that Todd is the one who's been assaulting those women. I mean, Todd is a suspect. He's gotten really weird over the years. I wouldn't put nothing past him."

"Yeah. That may be true, and I don't put nothing past anyone either, but I don't get why they wanted to interrogate Ann!"

"Maybe she's part of the plot."

"Yeah. But I doubt that, though."

They were silent momentarily while Shane rang up another customer.

"It has to be a white guy doing those crimes because black folks are not that flamboyant with rapes."

"Whoa!" Shane became defensive. "That was absolutely a racist statement. What if I say white folks don't eat fried chicken and watermelon at hood parties, always be late for work, listen to jungle music—"

"Let's see." Mark thought for a second then called the names out as he counted them on his fingers. "Son of

Sam, the Zodiac Killer, Jack the Ripper, Jeffrey Dahmer, and Ted Bundy. And guess what? All of these rednecks are white. Just like Charles Manson and that crazy lady Aileen Wuornos."

Shane was heated like a fire-breathing dragon now. He couldn't play it off as if he was cool. He felt Mark was pulling a race card. "Let's just change the subject," he said angrily. "I don't want to talk about that anymore."

"Okay, fine, then. I have to make a run later on, and I want you to ride with me."

"I have no problem traveling with you to your destination. Besides…Todd and Ann should be here later on to close the store, but can you at least tell me where we headed?"

"Nope! It's a secret."

"I'm not good with secrets." Shane said sarcastically. "Hopefully, you're about to take me shopping." He smiled.

"Pssst!" Mark looked him up and down and declared with twisted lips, "Man, you're not my woman. What do I look like, taking another guy shopping? You must be kidding."

Shane threw his arms up in the air, then yelled. "It was worth taking a shot at. Can you blame a guy for trying?"

"No, I can't, but let me assure you that you got the right game but the wrong man."

Chapter 33

C ause it's all in my head. I think about it over and over again. And I can't keep picturing you with him. And it hurts so bad."

Tim McGraw and Nelly's hit song played through the speakers of the Mazda.

"And I can't take it and I can't shake it, no!" Captain Smith sang along to the music in his deep country voice.

Miranda turned the volume down with the remote and laughed. "I can't believe you're over there howling like a dog. You are going to scare all of the hogs away."

"Leave me alone. I'm in my own zone." He smiled while bobbing his head from side to side then manually turned the music back up.

"If you are going to let the music play, then leave it to the professionals because the way you sound, you must keep your day job. There is no room for you in the music industry or on Broadway."

They both giggled together as their vehicle made a right onto Eighth Street. Every lead in the investigation into the auto store turned into a blank mission. The entire bureau had been hitting the streets on foot and turning blocks in unmarked cars to search for the slightest suspicion.

After minutes of joking around, Smith turned the stereo

back down then glared at his long-term friend. "I have a confession to make," he said with his serious face on. He paused for a minute in the hope that Miranda would give him an indication not to spill the beans, but he was biting. He had her full attention. "The reason why I have been spending nights at the office is because my wife and I decided to separate. I figured if I stayed away from home for a while, then she would begin missing me and beg me to come back.

She looked into his eyes with great concern as she turned her entire body towards him.

"However, my game plan didn't work. She filed for divorce and had a special prosecutor to deliver them to my office. After I received the subpoena for court, I went to the house to see if we could reconcile or at least let me change her mind for the time being." He cut off his words mid-sentence as tears welled in his eyes. His lips began vibrating uncontrollably.

She rubbed the back of his head to calm him down. Knowing that compassion would also edge him on with more information.

"She must have forgotten that I still had a key to our own home." He wiped his nose then sniffed. "When I opened the door. I heard some strange noises that sounded like some type of wild animal. So I crept upstairs to find my wife in the bed with another man." He cried like a little baby.

Miranda hugged him but jumped when the car began swerving and almost ran head-on into a diesel truck. The vehicle came to a complete stop on the side of the road, and Captain Smith dried his eyes out. He quickly hopped out of the vehicle then ran a couple feet before he fell on his knees.

Miranda ran after him then covered his body with her body. "I'm so sorry to hear that," she whispered in his ear.

"I can't believe this happened in our own home." He beat the ground with the palm of his hands. "And to make things worse, it's my neighbor. I thought that he was my friend."

"Everything will be all right." She massaged his shoulders and back. "I'm here for you. We will get through this together like everything else we have conquered."

"Why does everybody always say that everything is going to be all right?"

"I guess…because that's all we know to say. I mean… what else must I say?"

"Just be honest for Christ's sake!" He raised up off the ground then wiped the dirt and tiny rocks from his pant leg.

"Well, if you want me to be honest, I knew something was going on, but it wasn't my place to say anything."

"What?" He sounded angry. "You knew my wife was cheating. Come on now! You must have more faith in me than that. I would definitely tell you if I knew. I didn't have to see it to have proof. You must not forget that women have what is called a woman's intuition. It's in our genes to discern certain things."

"I understand." He pulled himself together.

"I guess the only thing that I can do. I must find a way to move on with my life. I know it's going to be hard at first but eventually I will get over it."

Chapter 34

lass was nearly over, but just like any other pregnant woman, Denise had to urinate frequently. She crossed her legs back and forth in the chair several times before she decided to excuse herself. She got out of the seat and raised up one finger like she was in the church choir or something.

She walked out of the group's section and headed past the entrance area towards the restroom. It was quiet and cold. She thought she heard a creepy noise, so she turned and saw a shadow standing in the darkness of her path. Immediately she was frightened. The figure reminded her of the shape of the man that raped her months ago. She fell to the ground, and with a loud voice, she screamed out.

Her voice traveled through all four corners of the building. Sherie and the rest of the ladies heard her and instantly stopped what they were doing. They all ran out of the room in their protective mode. They felt like mother ducks fearing for her duckling's life.

Angie, Leslie, and Aileena made it to the scene first. Afterwards, Sherie, Kreasha, and Asa arrived to help their friend get up off the ground. The first load of women attacked the unknown man. They karate-chopped his head

"You are not supposed to be in here!" one of them angrily yelled.

The man covered his body with his arms and hands to be shielded from as many of the blows as he could. The women were attacking him so wildly to the point that they nearly ripped his black-on-black windbreakers off him. They swung as hard as they could with every punch and every kick. This man reminded them so much of their worst enemy.

Sherie finally got a chance to observe the commotion after she assisted Denise. "Hey!" She screamed. "Stop!"

Nobody listened to her. They kept doing what they were doing until she yelled again as hard as she could. "Please stop it. Stop it. Everyone just stop it!" She was very emotional. Next, she placed both of her hands on the top of her head then breathed out heavily.

Everyone knew when enough was enough. She now had their undivided attention.

"Get back." She motioned with her arms to separate the crowd. "Back away," she demanded, and they complied. "Ladies! This is my boyfriend. His name is Mark Pryor. He is here to pick me up from work because my car wouldn't start earlier."

Mark smiled sarcastically then waved his fingers at the women.

"Oh!" one of them said, but all of the women were embarrassed. Denise was ashamed the most because she was the one who started the confrontation.

"I'm so sorry, Marcus," Angie said then adjusted his collar.

"Mark...my name is not Marcus. It's Mark."

"I'm so sorry, then, Mark. How can I ever repay you?"

"This is all my fault," Leslie admitted. "I should have never attacked you."

"It's okay. There are no hard feelings. You sure are a tough group of women."

"Yeah. We girls like to stick together."

"Please forgive us, Sherie," they all asked her individually. "No problem. We all know that it was a misunderstanding."

"I know, right?"

Everyone was silent until Sherie spoke up. "Well, I believe that we've all had enough for the day. Class is dismissed until next week."

The ladies all said their goodbyes then stepped outside after Sherie cut the lights off. Mark watched as each person got into their car then drove away. Mark turned to face his girlfriend and was about to mention what happened a few minutes before, but he noticed that Denise was still standing outside with them. He cut his eyes towards her so that Sherie would be aware.

"Oh. Hi! I didn't realize that you were still here."

"Yeah. I'm still here." She smiled. "My ride would usually have been here by now." Denise dialed numbers on her mobile, but the call went straight to voicemail.

"You can catch a ride with us if you want to?"

"No. I'm okay. I don't want to be too big of a burden on nobody." She dialed the same number again to no avail.

"You're not a burden at all. It would be my delight to drop you off at home. Besides, I can't just leave you out here all alone."

The night was kind of chilly outside, and the breeze was blowing. Nobody noticed, but Denise had actually urinated on herself when she fell on the floor. She didn't want to cause too much attention to the wetness on her pants. She looked down at her cellular phone and stared, then said "Well…okay," as the pee began to freeze up on her leg.

"Good. Come on."

When the three of them headed towards the car, Shane hopped out of the front seat and got into the back.

"Who is that?" Sherie pointed and asked.

"Oh. This is my friend Shane." Mark said after all the doors slammed shut.

"Hi, everybody." He waved.

"Hey," the ladies responded.

"I'm surprised you don't remember him. He works at the auto store with me."

Sherie turned her neck to get a good view. "Oh. That's your manager. How have you been doing, Shane?"

"I'm all right. How are you?"

Chapter 35

FOUR MONTHS LATER…
It was the beginning of spring, but Captain Smith was doing a little bit more than spring cleaning. He was taking the last of his property out of the house that he once owned. The lawyers on both sides had finalized the divorce after the Smiths came to an agreement.

Of course his now ex-wife won the house – even with all of their kids being fully grown. Additionally, she was blessed with a fat monthly paycheck for alimony. She claimed since she never really worked because of the captain, she should be allowed to keep up with the lifestyle that she always lived.

Smith slowly descended the long staircase, and a million and one memories ran through his mind. He was sad to be leaving behind what he had built to another man. Plus, the queen of his castle betrayed him, and he wasn't able to foresee the clues. He guessed he was too caught up in his work after all, like she had constantly claimed.

He kept his head forward along with the box in his hands as he walked past his ex and her now fiancé. He was disturbed during the whole moving process because they both stood at the door with their arms crossed. To make the situation worse, they didn't say a word to him.

They mugged him the entire time like he was the one in the wrong or, perhaps, they were just in a hurry for him to leave, so they could get on with their infatuation.

The captain didn't feel like a captain anymore. He felt like a pirate getting robbed as he opened passenger side door of the Mustang then got in. He reclined the seat far back to allow space for the mess in the back. He next directed his pitiful face towards the driver.

"I told you that I have your back through this rough time. You can depend on me if you can't depend on anybody else. You don't ever have to worry about me bringing this situation up again or using it against you," Miranda informed him.

"Thanks, Miranda." A tear fell from his eye. "Our business is our business, and it's not to be heard.

"Right!" She pulled straight out of the driveway.

"The guys at work probably wouldn't respect me anymore if they find out that I can't run my own house but I try to control an entire department."

"Authority has nothing to do with a relationship. But if I ever get married, please remind me to get a prenuptial agreement because people like your wife have no heart."

"Ex-wife," he murmured.

Chapter 36

For the last three or four months, it seemed as if Denise's house had been haunted. She didn't know if she was tripping or what, but every other day, it was like different items in her house were misplaced or removed from the spot where she put them.

However, she ignored the strange disappearances because she didn't want to stress herself out. The baby was growing inside her stomach and appeared to be tossing and turning.

She had to get her mind on more positive things, so she grabbed the mammogram off the kitchen counter that had been snapped at the doctor's office earlier that day. She screenshot it, then posted it on Facebook and Instagram to see how many likes and comments she would get.

Next, she went into the room to check on Danny Boy. He was sound asleep, so she stood at the door, smiled, then cut the light back off. She rubbed her belly while walking into the living room. She picked up her phone to call her sister. They talked until Denise fell asleep.

LATER THAT NIGHT...

Denise was awakened by footsteps and the sound of rambling. It seemed like she had some kind of inherent mother's intuition, even when sleeping, able to hear abstract noises. At first, she thought it was a raccoon because they were normal in that neck of the woods, but she decided to get up and check anyway because the creature was persistent and distracting.

She reluctantly got out of bed and followed the trail of the noise. Unbeknownst to her, it was right in her backyard. She peeked out the window, and, to her surprise, it wasn't a raccoon going through her trash. It wasn't any kind of animal at all. It was a human being digging deep down in her trashcan. He had one hand full of papers, and the other hand was all the way at the bottom of the barrel. She couldn't believe her eyes. She nearly went into panic mode but took a deep breath and took back control of her fear.

She went to the window, unlocked it, then roughly raised it up. Her idea was to make sure that the trespasser heard it. She believed he didn't hear because he looked towards her direction but didn't bulge.

Whether she knew it or not, the unknown man wasn't anxious to leave even if he did get identified. He knew that it was dark outside, and he knew that it would be approximately three minutes by the time a call was made to 911 and even longer until the units arrived. He had already tested and timed his discovery by recently making a prank phone call to the precinct.

"Hey!" she finally yelled out. "Get out of my yard. I'm about to call the police."

By the time that Denise flicked the light switch on, the stranger looked up, stuffed his pants with the papers that he had in his hands, then took off. He ran so fast that he stumbled and then tripped over his own feet. He jumped up off the ground with the palm of his hands, bloody knees, and scuffled up elbows. He didn't mind the bruises, though. He got what he went to get, so that information was more valuable than anything else.

Chapter 37

"Today, I will be preaching out of the book of Prov-
erbs. We should all know where it says that beauty
fades and charm is deceit." The pastor taught in his
powerful voice.

"Ooo-weeeee," two elderly women exclaimed then
yanked their heads back as if the Holy Ghost had hit them.
They were the type of women who put on a performance
at every church service. If the preacher made sense or not,
it was like community theater with all the dramatics going
on in there.

"The reason why the spirit led Solomon to write this
particular passage in the Bible is because people look for
the beauty in everything and every person, but everything
that looks good isn't good for you. We must realize that
even Satan transformed himself into an angel before he
was kicked out of heaven and cast down like a speeding
lightning bolt."

"Yes, Lord! Thank you, Jesus!" The two elderly ladies
waved their hands in the air from side to side. They were
always in a competition with each other to see who could
show out the most.

"Now, I am not saying that I shouldn't have a nice-looking wife or you shouldn't have a handsome husband. But

what I am saying is that if beauty is all that you are looking for in a person then that relationship won't last because one day that beauty will fade away. The only thing that will be everlasting on this earth is the word of God. That long curly hair will draw up or fall out. That pretty smile can become crooked. That figure that is shaped like an hourglass or Barbie doll will gain weight or lose weight, and that gorgeous face will wrinkle."

"Hallelujah, Hallelujah!" Mrs. Hattie Mae yelled then fell on the floor.

Thelma looked down at Hattie Mae and saw her hat on the carpet as she rolled around. She mumbled under her breath. Thelma and Hattie Mae had known each other for a very long time. They went to school together, and now they were both seventy-two years old. They always competed against each other since their cheerleading days. Now, even at this old age, Thelma wasn't going to let little Mrs. Hattie Mae beat her at anything. Thelma lost focus on what her pastor was saying. She didn't even hear his last words. Whatever he said last didn't matter. She hopped on the floor next to her friend, then she laid down and moved her arms and legs back and forth across the floor as if she was trying to make an imprint or an angel in the snow. "Amen!" she yelled out as loud as she could. "Thank you, Jesus!" she declared then said something that she didn't know what the words were herself. All she knew what that it sounded like she was talking in Hebrew or speaking in tongues.

Most of the members of the church didn't pay too much attention to the ladies. They were already used to their episodes because they put on a show all the time.

The preacher kept preaching. He didn't know whether the women were faking or not. All he thought about was the word his wife had coined – "church rats". It was something like "hood rats" except that church rats preferred to mess around and eat their cheese in the church instead of in the projects.

Hattie Mae And Thelma finally decided to pick themselves up off the ground. On their way up, they bumped into each other and nearly knocked one another back down. Luckily, one of their high heels had twisted just enough to be balanced on the floor. Thelma caught hold of Hattie Mae then they wiggled together to plop down on the pews.

"Now that was good exercise." Thelma dug in her purse to retrieve some paper then used it to fan herself.

"I know what you mean, girl. I am exhausted, tired, aching and some more things."

"I know that's right!" she huffed then wiped the sweat off her nose and forehead.

Thelma didn't say anything for another minute. She sat there, breathing heavily. Her chest was rapidly moving in and out. She thought her heart was about to burst because it was pumping so fast.

"Do you hear the lesson the pastor is teaching on today? I believe he's preaching that for these young girls in this church that walk around flaunting their stuff. They got them big ol' booties and all that makeup on. Chile, only if they knew that all of their looks are not going to last that long."

"Yeah. They better cherish it while they can. Then the guys be trying to be really charming, and charm is deceitful like the pastor says."

Hattie Mae slid over closer to her friend so she could whisper, "You know I heard that Deacon Charles has been cheating on his wife."

"You don't say!" Thelma was shocked. She adjusted her glasses on her nose. "Tell me more!"

The pastor stopped his message for a moment then glanced over to eyeball the two members who just happened to be Thelma and Hattie Mae. He didn't have to look too far
because they were both sitting on the front row.

Immediately they were silenced. They didn't want to cause any disturbance between the gospel or the Lord's house. The duo sat there quietly and gave their undivided attention to the orator.

When the pastor quit scolding the two with his eyes, he continued on with the service. After a few minutes, Hattie Mae's bladder began to erupt within her. She squeezed her insides tightly in the hope of controlling the urination, but it was too overwhelming. She squirmed her legs from side to side because she wanted to stay put in order to hear the reverend's message. Unfortunately, she couldn't hold it any longer, so she rose up slowly, making sure not to drip a tinkle because, at her age, leakage was highly possible.

Thelma observed her friend as Hattie Mae put one finger up to excuse herself then went on to the restroom area.

By the time she made it inside the stall, she wiped the seat with some wipes that she always kept inside her purse. She cleaned herself then opened the bathroom stall door to a surprise.

A man met her before she could step out. He had on all

dark clothes with a ski mask to match the colors of his outfit. Hattie Mae was about to scream, but he used his huge
hands to cover her mouth then dragged her back into the
stall. She made several attempts to wrestle with the devil,
but he quickly debilitated her fragile body. He had a tight
clutch on her mouth, and his fingers were poking into her
jawbone.

Hattie Mae didn't know was going on. She'd never been
in a type of situation like this before. Everything had
always gone the way she wanted it to since she was a tod-
dler. Now the unimaginable was about to happen, and she
didn't have any control over it.

The masked man ran his loose hand down to her hun-
dred-year-old brown stocking then into her diaper. An
odor released from out of nowhere. It smelled like pork
rinds, stale Cheetos and onions all mixed together.

She made another attempt to struggle with this fleshly
demon. She squeezed her legs as tight as she could then
tried to remove his hand to no avail. It was like she was
wrestling with a supernatural being or higher power
because of the strength. He grabbed her by her throat then
began to choke the life out of her. He was not remorse-
ful at all while she swallowed her own spit. Her stockings
were now ruined, and the diaper fell to the floor. Next, he
slammed her body into the wooden stall door frame. Their
bodies took up the whole space.

While her back was on the floor, he spread her legs then
yanked the lower half of her body up towards him. Just
as he was about to pull his pants down, the door to the
restroom opened, and he heard the high-heel footsteps.

"I had to come in here and join you, Mrs. Hattie Mae."

Thelma looked in the mirror to make sure her wig and makeup were still intact. "All of that rolling around on the floor off-set my linens." She adjusted the crease in her dress. "Yeah, honey, baby, chile, the Holy Ghost really got to me this time. Turning and tossing on that darn carpet made my undies go all in my crotch and booty hole. I may need to check them to make sure I ain't go no brown runs in my panties."

The masked man tried to be quiet as a church house mouse, but he lost his footing and made a squeaking noise.

"Hattie Mae, are you listening to me?" She turned to see what the strange sound was then walked toward the stalls. She vaguely heard grunts and a moan, then noticed a hand hanging out on the floor. She opened the door and screamed when she saw the villain and her defenseless half-naked friend.

The unknown man panicked then let go of Hattie's limp body. He jabbed his fist into Thelma's nose, and she quickly fell to floor. He couldn't believe his own reaction to the episode. It took him a split second to collect his thoughts, then he climbed out the same window that he came in through.

Chapter 38

After everyone was settled in their comfortable seats, Sherie didn't waste any time to speak. "Unfortunately, this will be our last meeting. The government funding has run out for our sessions."

"Oh, no!" The class attendants all mourned.

"It probably was just a front anyway like they really cared about us," Denise vented. "The government only care about itself. The least of their worries are people they don't know."

"Just like FEMA ran out of funds for all of those innocent people affected by the Katrina storm. They leave us stranded, helpless and defenseless," Asa said.

"Ladies!" Sherie did her signature move by crossing her left leg over the right. "We still have to be positive. Remember we cannot achieve positive results with negativity."

"You are so right. So, on another note, then....I must admit that I really enjoyed you gals and your company. I feel like I have gained more than a handful of brand new friends."

"I agree, and I hope that we can all exchange numbers later," someone else added.

"Most definitely! We can exchange numbers." They all

stood side by side.

Leslie raised her hand then waited for a moment to stop before she said what was on her mind. "Not to get onto the government's back again, but I want to know what made America vote Dummy Trump as president?"

Many of the ladies laughed at her comment.

"That is y'all's president," Kreasha said, then smacked her lips. "I am not a democrat or a republican. I am an independent. So, this is y'all's America, not mine!"

"President Dummy Trump just may make America great again like he said he would."

"Psssttt! That clown lies about everything with a straight face. America just fell into a reprobate mind like the Bible says. They deceived themselves because they didn't want crooked Hillary as President and Bill Clinton being the First Lady."

"You mean the first gentleman?" Angie corrected her.

"No, I mean Bill Clinton would have been the First Lady. Crooked Hillary would have been getting head in the White House like her husband did then made him wear the panties. Monica Lewinsky wouldn't be trying to suck on Bill anymore. Monica would have been attempting to lick on Hillary."

Sherie patiently waited for her clients to finish chuckling. She was thinking, if they only knew how serious this meeting is about to get. She understood that sometimes one is compelled to choose between two separate evils. When that happens, do you pick the greater or lesser evil?

One by one, the crowd observed that Sherie was acting abnormal with a distinctive expression on her face, so they gave her back the floor.

She pondered for a little while longer to collect her thoughts together. "Um. I have something important that I want to share with you divas." She stumbled over her words. "Someone made a comment before about why I chose the career that I did. They figured that I didn't know your pain or that I couldn't assimilate and sympathize with your feelings." Sherie ran her eyes around the room to see if she had everyone's undivided attention. After she realized that the ladies were following her speech, she continued. "I want you all to know that my baby boy is my son and my brother."

They were confused. That statement went over their heads.

"Let me elucidate so you can catch my drift." She lifted her chin up to space then rephrased her confession. "I gave birth to a little boy named Marcus. Since I birthed him, then that means he is my son. My dad is the father of Marcus, so he is also my brother."

There was complete silence for several minutes as each individual's eyes were filled with tears. They couldn't believe their own ears. If their lives were a nightmare then it must be hell for Sherie.

"Oh my God!" The crowd was very emotional.

Angie couldn't contain her eruption any longer. She ran as fast as she could then dove upon Sherie in a friendly manner. She gave her the biggest hug ever then they all followed. It was like one hopeful family, bonding together in a group.

Sherie hated reliving her past, but if that was what assisted others, then so be it. "When I was a little girl, my own biological father used to come into the room when my mother was gone, or when she was sleeping, to molest me." She cried. "I felt ashamed for so many years to tell anyone then, one day, when I finally built up enough courage to tell my mother, she didn't even believe me. I have dealt with this sinful nature for so long. I couldn't give my baby up for an adoption, and I couldn't have an abortion. I just felt that killing an innocent baby wouldn't be the correct thing to do. He didn't ask to be conceived, no matter how he came about."

Denise felt what she was saying more than anybody. After all, she was pregnant with this unknown rapist's baby. She rubbed her navel on her belly because it was starting to poke out.

All the rest of the ladies broke up their circle after sobbing and bonding for several minutes. They each wobbled back to their chairs like they were half-dead. Sherie's story sucked the life out of them.

Asa let everyone calm down a little bit before she drew all attention to herself. "I have a confession that I would like to make also. I know that what I have to say will inspire another intervention, but it's something that I've been having on my mind for a long, long time now." She spoke in her Asian accent, which everyone understood perfectly. "Me believe that I was the first to get raped because I didn't hear about it much before I did. This person must have been an amateur at the time because he didn't wear a mask like he did with you all. Therefore, I saw him face and me can't get him features out of my head."

"Did you ever let the police know this information?"

"No, me didn't." Asa was sad.

"If you saw his face vividly, then I believe that could be

valuable evidence for the authorities. Maybe they can have you pick his photo out of a lineup or something."

"You think so?"

"Yes! Most definitely!"

"Me will go to the police in the morning then."

Her friends smiled because the slightest hope of justice meant a snippet of relief for them.

Chapter 39

I refuse to let these tragedies continue in my home state. This is our city. We run this so why are these crimes perpetually going on right under our noses?"

Captain Smith didn't let his team get settled in well before he started his lecture. As a matter of fact, a few his officers were just coming through the door.

"So, the question is what are we doing to prevent further occurrences?" he asked angrily into the crowd. He was monitoring everyone's actions and attempting to read their minds. "Obviously nothing." He grabbed a stack full of papers then threw them everywhere. Next, he grabbed a book then slammed it against the wall.

The people in the room were terrified. They had seen their boss mad many times before, but he had never been this mean. Some stooped down in their chairs while others dodged the items he threw.

"We are not doing anything at all because it hasn't stopped. Our technology and intelligence level are too sophisticated to let someone outfox us." He walked up on a rookie agent, then had an eyeball-to-eyeball stand-off with him.

"So what are your plans for this bureau? What has your

game plan been thus far?" He pointed his finger sternly at the guy while grilling him simultaneously.

"Uh. Nothing. I just…" He was scared.

"Wrong answer! You are fired. Get out of my building." Captain Smith meant every word he said. "You can appeal my decision to the commissioner board if you like, but as of now, you are terminated!"

The man couldn't believe his ears. He'd only been working in the rape division for a few months. He slowly leaned out of his seat, grabbed his property from the desk, then walked out of the room, shocked.

Captain Smith had everyone's attention more than ever now. The committee was paranoid. They didn't want to lose their jobs.

"Ladies and gentlemen. What I'm about to show you are the people that have been torn apart by this stalking rapist. All we have now are DNA samples that have been collected through forensics, and so far all of the DNA belongs to one individual." Agent Thompson took over the conversation before the meeting got too far out of hand. "However, since this guy apparently has no criminal history, he is not in our database. So, we must do what we can to hunt the hunter down and find this John Doe." She then went to pick up the remote control for the projector and turned the screen on. "These are all the victims of violence so far." She hit the button to bring up each picture.

"The first to ever report to the local police was Asa Gagliard. Then Leslie Strong, Angie Stone, Denise Brown, Kreasha Otis, Aleena Santiago, and this pervert went so far as to attempt an attack on a transgender by the name of Ricky Minaj."

"Aw. Ummmm. Excuse me." A senior officer raised her hand. "Do you mean Nicky Minaj like the iconic rapper?"

"No! This guy feels that he is as sexy as her. He may have named himself after her, but he goes by Ricky Minaj."

"Oh!"

All the attention in the building was slowly directed towards Agent Ross. He was in lala land, with both of his hands propped against his cheeks. He was drooling and google-eyeing the ladies on the screen.

"I think that they had the right guy when they arrested him," one of the agents whispered to another one.

"Now, people. We are well-trained feds, so let's act like it and have this guy captured by the end of the week," Thompson concluded.

Captain Smith was still pacing the floor in an outrage. "Why are you still in here, people?" He yelled. "Go get some work done!"

After the group left the room rapidly, Thompson and Smith didn't waste any time to give recognition to what they noticed. "Did you see the way Agent Ross was sobbing over the women on the screen?" she inquired.

"Yes. I did. I was just about to say something to you about that."

"What do you think that we should do about his abnormal and insubordinate actions?"

"Assign another special deputy to trail his every movement. Make sure the special agent doesn't let him out of his sight. When he goes to the bathroom to use it, I want to know what color is on the tissue when he wipes between his butt cheeks."

Chapter 40

Asa pulled up into Nashville's Eighth Precinct early in the morning. She was skeptical about filing a report with the local authorities. In her country, the police collaborated with the criminals.

"May I help you?" an elderly black lady asked her.

"Yes. I'm here to file a report."

"What type of report, ma'am?"

"Someone broke into my house and sexually assaulted me some time ago."

"Okay, then, ma'am. Since the rape charge will supersede the burglary charge, I'll contact the rape division, and, in return, they will inform me when they are ready to see you."

Obviously still shaken up, she inquired, "What am I supposed to do until then?"

The dispatcher handed Asa a brown clipboard with a stack full of paperwork on it. "Fill out as much information that you can possibly get adequately. Everything doesn't have to be politically correct. But it does have to be reachable." She then pointed to the benches that were preoccupied. "Until you are called, please have a seat over there."

After forty-five minutes of seeing traffic flow in and out of the police department, Asa was finally called to the back. She didn't know what she was about to reveal or what would be the end result of this voyage. But somewhere during the process of waiting, she lost all hope in any type of closure.

"How are you doing, Ms. Gagliardi?"

"I could be better."

"Situations like this are never easy. But this is the first step to being healed. My name is Lieutenant Henderson, and I'm here to help you start overcoming this catastrophe. I have reviewed your paperwork, and I see that you stated in your report that this incident occurred almost a year ago."

"Correct," Asa agreed. She was rocking back and forth in the padded chair.

"Why didn't you come in to report it back then?"

"I was hysterical. For a long while, I was dead to the world. It was like my soul had been captured and all of the life was sucked out of me." She clutched her purse tighter to her chest. "I laid there on the floor for hours and stared at the ceiling. I literally couldn't move at all."

"I understand." Lieutenant Henderson flipped through the paperwork again. This time, she only paid attention to certain marked sections. "Did you get a good look at this perp?"

"Yes, I did. He was in my house. We were face to face to each other."

"Could you identify him if you ever saw him again?"

"I'm positive that I can." Asa was almost hyperventilating. "I will never forget his face. I can still see him vividly to this day."

"Well, that's good!" Lieutenant Henderson exclaimed strongly.

Asa glared at her incredulously. She couldn't believe what was supposed to be so good about seeing a criminal in her house.

The lieutenant noticed the disgusted look on her face, so she replied, "Nah. Honey." She giggled then waved her hand dismissively. "I didn't mean to insinuate that it was good for a criminal to be in your home. What I meant was to say was that since you can give us a positive identification of this guy, then you can help us capture him. And what is good about it is that another predator will be apprehended and taken off the streets."

"Okay. Perfect."

"The way that this operation is normally processed is by a photo lineup of maybe five to six people. The victim comes down here to pick their attacker out of the photo lineup, and we go from there. But since we don't have any ideas of who this man may be, we can only ask you to give us a description of the culprit, and we will have the regional news share the information."

"So, will my name be mentioned in the media?"

"Yes." She winced. Asa was reluctant to put her image out there. "I must remind you that this is a very serious issue. But the question remains…are you willing to go through this procedure that will give you closure and maybe also help to prevent future violations?"

"Absolutely." She clutched the handle on her purse then buckled her knees. "At first I was concerned about my character getting damaged by the television stations. But I can't cope with this any longer. On one hand, I run the risk of ruining my political credentials. But then on the other hand, I have closure and the ability to help others."

"What have you decided to do?"

"I decided that I have to put my political ties to the side and come forward with the truth because I don't want this guy hurting anyone else." She put her head down then started weeping again. "I swear I don't."

"What do you mean by saying that you don't want this guy to hurt anyone else?" Her eyes enlarged as she scooted forward in her chair. "Do you know this guy?"

"No."

"Do you have any information about the attacks on others?"

"As a matter of fact, I believe that I do. I informed you earlier that I was sexually assaulted some time ago. But I never told you about how long ago."

"Well, now would be the best time for you to tell me, Ms. Gagliardi."

"I was raped on May 11, 2012."

"Wow! That's like eleven maybe going on twelve months ago. Tell me what made you come forward now."

"I believe that this guy who raped me is the same one who's been in the news for years."

"You mean the one they labeled as Stalker Man?"

"Yes."

"First off, for the past five years, I've been having my woman's intuition telling me that's him every time that I turn on the news station. And second, I've been attending these sexual abuse classes, and these same ladies who were assaulted all talk as if we've been attacked by the same guy."

"You mean like some of the details or tactics that this guy used are similar to the others' attacks?"

"Exactly. The only difference is that I believe that I was the first one that he raped. He must have been new to his sickness and forgot to wear a mask or maybe he noticed that he didn't cover his face with me. And that's when maybe he began to wear a costume."

"Are you sure?"

"Yes."

"This is what we need!" Lieutenant Henderson stood to her feet and took the phone from off the hook. "What I'm about to do is call our artist. His name is Calvin Bland. He is very proficient with his artwork. Anyone that you ask him to draw, he will draw them perfectly. He will enhance their facial features to fit their age if years have passed like in your case."

"Will this take long?"

"No, he is quick but brilliant."

She pressed the buttons to dial Calvin's extension. When he answered the phone, she spoke in a rushing manner. "Can you please hurry down here right now with the case of the century? Your assistance is highly required."

After the lieutenant hung up the phone with him, he was knocking at her door within three minutes.

"Come in." She obliged him. "This is the guy I was telling you about."

"Hi." He waved at the ladies. "Anybody need a portrait drawn?"

Asa waved back, but her bashfulness kind of forced her to duck down into the seat. "Yes. I guess I do," she said shyly.

"Mr. Bland, will you show her your office and take really good care of her?"

"I sure will." He looked at Asa then used his hands to guide her out the door.

By the time an hour passed, Ms. Gagliardi had given Calvin enough details to sketch up the matching resemblance of the man that had taken advantage of her months before.

She stared at the picture then began to cry. She was determined that the face in front of her was the same face that had been in her head since that heinous day in May.

Now it was time for the villain behind the mask to get exposed. He was always introduced through the media as the notorious rapist with the unknown face. Unfortunately for him, Asa had just given the world a game changer.

Chapter 41

The whole world was listening when the breaking news was aired. Never before had a single broadcast given so many people relief and resentment at the same time. Among the people viewing the news channel were officers all over the world. Captain Smith and Lieutenant Thompson just happened to be side by side in a local gas station. The excitement was so intense, Captain Smith dropped his cup of joe on the floor. His mouth was wide open as he stared at the smart tv that hung on the wall. All his lady friend could do was shake her head in disgrace at the drawing of someone the two knew recognized immediately. It took a few minutes for the duo to gather their thoughts but once they did, they gave each other a fist bump then a smile. The artist scribbled the sketch perfectly.

Chapter 42

While the media gave millions of people something to wonder about, Captain Smith and his sidekick were pulling up at his old house. They were relaxed because they didn't have to put the clues together. The dots connected by themselves. They were more in tune with this transition than anybody else.

For the first time ever, it took the man longer than it took the woman to get out of the car. Smith had to adjust to the butterflies that were swarming around in his belly. Thompson checked her glock 17 just to make sure that a round was loaded in the chamber. Smith wiped the sweat beads that formed around his forehead, neck and nose. Next, he joined his long-term teammate in pursuit of an infidel.

Smith looked around the house cautiously as he approached the front door. He made himself pay close attention to the windows to make sure there weren't any sudden movements going on in the home.

He knew that his ex-wife always kept a spare key underneath the third rock in the flower garden. Sometimes, she never even locked the door because of her comfort in the neighborhood. However, he knew he couldn't just barge in for search and seizure protocols.

Thompson tapped on the door then stood to the side.

The door was opened instantly, and the pair brushed past the captain's ex-wife.

"What are you doing in my home? You know you don't live here anymore. We settled this in court, remember?" She nagged then tried to restrain him.

He yanked away and headed towards the kitchen. Thompson accidentally-on-purpose bumped into the woman as she followed him.

Tim's eyes were bucked when he finally noticed the captain stampeding in his direction. Smith didn't waste any time to wrestle him to the floor then handcuff him.

"What are you doing to my fiancé?" Martha screamed hysterically. "Leave him alone! You are just mad because I don't want you anymore. If you was half the man that Tim is, then it may be a micro chance that we would still be together. But you are selfish, inconsiderate, and only leave me at home alone. So, it's over!"

Miranda moved to block Martha from touching her boss. It was a tussle at first, but Miranda finally got the best of her.

"You two have to leave my house right now. If not, then I am going to file a restraining order on both of you for harassment." Martha continued her rant.

Smith yanked Tim off the ground with one hand. No one in the house knew what was going on except for the FBI agents. Neither of them responded. They led Tim through the huge house until they returned to the living room.

"This is why I always watch the news channel. Do you remember asking me why I was so committed to the news?"

Martha had a dumbfounded expression on her face. "What does this have to do with anything?"

Smith grabbed the remote control off the table then cut the television on. To their surprise, Tim's face was on every channel that he flicked to.

Martha was so ashamed. Tim was shocked to see a perfectly drawn picture of him. He couldn't do anything but put his head down in defeat. After all this time, he thought he was slick and winning. He didn't ever believe that his rampage would end. The saying must be true: "All things will catch up with you.

Chapter 43

Tim was sitting in the interrogation room. He was paranoid and cold from the steel seat that he was on. And what made things worse was that his arms were handcuffed tightly behind his back. It had been hours since he had been isolated in the small area. However, he noticed the tinted window that he couldn't see out of, but he knew that whoever was watching him could see in. This was just a strategy called the waiting game to see if the suspect would crack.

After a while longer of the cuffs cutting off his circulation, Captain Smith finally came into the room and sat across from him. "You are a very popular man, Mr. Timothy Douglas." He threw a thick folder onto the table. "You have ruined many lives, so you have to compensate for that with your own life."

"I have no idea what you are talking about," Timothy responded angrily.

"Let's cut to the chase. If you are willing to submit to a DNA test and pass with flying colors, then you can go scott-free. But we both know that you are not going to do that because you didn't use protection when you were raping these innocent women. Your semen is all over the place. We have jars of your DNA in rape kits. So, basically, what I am saying is that it's over with. Your excursion has come to an end."

Tim was silent for a minute. His face was as pale as a ghost. He knew that the woman who gave the description of him was proof enough to convict him.

"Do you want to know what the flip side to this whole event is? I mean, what really made it so complicated to catch me was that I played the entire world by playing cat and mouse with you. Your wife—well, when she was your wife—used to brag about how good of an FBI agent you were."

Captain Smith relaxed in his seat as he took in the information that he was hearing.

"At first, I was like, 'Why is she telling me this? Nobody's supposed to know who the real FBI agents are'. You lied to me for so long and said that you were an electrical engineer. Then it dawned on me. Martha didn't have anybody to confide in, so she felt comfort in telling me all of y'all's personal business."

"Okay. I see," he replied nonchalantly.

"I also noticed that she wasn't getting any attention at home. Just for future reference, know that a woman who loves to talk needs a lot of attention, and if they are hyper, they need sex to calm them down, but in her words, you were too busy to realize that."

"We are not here to talk about my future or my past. We are rather here to talk about yours."

"Well. I never planned on getting caught." He leaned forward.

"Yeah, who does?"

"I figured that if I could get in Wifey's head then she

would get into yours and have you all discombobulated. And it worked, too. You must admit that she distracted you from your job. You couldn't think straight, therefore you had your whole department looking in all the wrong places. It's amazing how the things that you need to find are right under your nose, but you are too far-sighted to realize it."

"The only thing that I know is that you are going to spend the rest of your life behind bars, and they might even give you the lethal injection or electric chair."

Tim didn't pay attention to Smith's world. He had his own point that he wanted to get across. "Have you ever noticed how Martha squirms when you are deep up in her?"

He mimicked her actions. "Or did you listen to how she purrs right before her eyes roll in the back of her head? No. Wait! Maybe you haven't had an orgasm in so long because of how she exploded like a fire hydrant. She had fluids backed up for years."

The captain's face and palms were sweating. Anyone could tell that the suspect was pushing his buttons. Smith cleared his throat then adjusted his shirt and tie.

"And you want to know what the best part is?" Tim stood halfway up and whispered in the agent's ear. "She does wonders in my booty hole with that long, wet tongue of hers. We used to call it tossing the salad in our days, but the new generation calls it eating groceries."

Captain Smith was outraged. The blood rushed so quickly to his brain that the vessels were about to burst. She told him that she had only done him that way and wouldn't dare give another man their special treatment. He couldn't take it anymore. In an outrage, he hysterically launched upwards then grabbed the suspect by his neck and rammed it against the interrogation table. The cold steel met his cheek as his flesh ripped open. Blood gushed out of his open wound along with broken particles of his bones. He put up a decent fight, but his combat was useless because of the tight cuffs on his wrists.

The chief and his colleagues had seen and heard enough. They barged into the room and struggled to separate the two. It was a bloodbath in the middle of the floor.

"Now what?" Captain Smith screamed belligerently. "The big bad wolf can't hurt a real man. You can only attack vulnerable women. You are a poor excuse for any type of creature."

"Listen!" The chief motioned like he was chopping his own head off. "I am your boss, and I say that is enough of these shenanigans. What are you trying to do, give the department a lawsuit?"

"This guy won't live long enough to see a lawsuit." Captain Smith stared at his boss. "And he doesn't have to submit to DNA samples, either. Swipe some of the blood off the floor to see if any of it matches what we've taken from any of the rape victims. I am willing to bet your top dollar that it matches every single last one of them."

Every person in the building observed Smith as he walked away. They were all thinking the same thing – maybe he does have a good point.

Chapter 44

After months of going to preliminary hearings and filing motions, it was finally time for Timothy to get sentenced. He had petitioned for a speedy trial, so the state had him in the jury box within six months. It was a very sad and emotional jury trail. Families cried as each and every victim described the horror that they were exposed to.

Now it was January 12th, and the prisoner's van pulled up at the courthouse as scheduled. The windows were tinted, so nobody could see inside. It was loaded with guards transporting this special, protected felon. Like any other high-profile case, Mr. Douglas had on a bullet-proof vest similar to the ones that officers who escorted him wore.

Extra patrolmen were stationed around the courthouse because of the uproar and outrage on all of Mr. Douglas' court days. The judge put a gag order on the case, but that didn't stop the media from talking.

The van door slid open, and seven special agents hurried around the inmate. When Timothy stepped out, he was shackled and chained around his waist, ankles, and hands. He noticed hundreds of folks standing outside to see him as if he was the main attraction at the zoo or in a haunted house. The entire Mexican mafia was there, along with many other blacks, whites, and Asians. They all wanted to see him dead.

As the squad led the way into the entrance, Captain Smith just happened to look up into a nearby building's window. He noticed a reflection glint off the sun's rays, and his military instinct kicked in. He immediately threw the prisoner to the ground.

"Sniper on the roof!" he yelled, as a bullet made a gigantic hole in the brick wall. It missed Timothy's head by inches. The agents snatched him off the ground by his arms, legs, and back, then rushed him into the entrance of the building.

Once the judge received word that Mr. Douglas was in the courthouse, he didn't waste any time sending the bailiffs out to do their jobs.

"Will all rise for the honorable Judge Justice presiding," the senior bailiff announced.

Everyone in the courtroom stood up except for the defendant. He was found guilty weeks before and didn't have any respect for the judge, prosecutors, or his own lawyer.

"You may all be seated," Judge Justice said. Looking like he was from the Netherlands, he opened the bulk folder that was on his stand. "Will the defendant and his lawyer step forward?" He didn't wait for them to get stationed at the stand before he spoke again. "I heard about the incident that recently happened outside, so we will get this hearing over with as quickly as possible. In the case record of 08-408, you have been found guilty of multiple rape charges. There are only two sentences that can be handed down due to their gruesome nature, and those are either life in prison or death. Is there anything you would like to say to the court before being sentenced?"

"Yes, there is!"

He adjusted his shirt collar, and then his slacks. "I am asking for mercy from the court today...to spare my life because handing down a death sentence would be cruel and unusual punishment. I had a rough childhood that caused me to have mental issues. My behavior was determined by my psychological impairment along with drug abuse. I am sorry for my actions, and I want to apologize to each and every person who I have hurt." He scrolled his eyes around the room, hoping that his sentimental words would elicit sympathy. "If I could take everything back, then I would. I'm just hoping I can be forgiven, and, from this day forward, the wounds will begin to heal."

The judge took a moment to gather his thoughts together. Truthfully, he had his mind made up on the sentence he was going to hand out before he came into the courtroom, but he had to put on a show. He took a deep breath then fumbled through the rest of the documents before he began writing with a red ink pen.

"Due to the nature of your crimes and the repeated acts, this court will not have mercy on you. You didn't have sympathy when you barged into a church and attacked a helpless and defenseless elderly woman. Neither did you show remorse when you raped a young lady in front of her only child. You are a pathetic man, the epitome of scum. Your kind should be wiped out of the human race, and today I will set an example with you. I will send a message to the world that notorious felons will not be tolerated here in Nashville, Tennessee, or anywhere at all in America. Therefore, I sentence you to death!" The word "death" rolled off his tongue in slow-motion as he slammed the gavel on the wooden pad.

The entire world paused on Timothy. His spirit left him, and his heart fluttered. He couldn't believe his ears. This very moment was a nightmare for him. The courtroom was in an uproar. Everybody was happy except for the defendant. He couldn't do anything but drop his head and let tears well up in his eyes.

"Get this nincompoop out of my courtroom," the judge yelled to the bailiffs. They quickly grabbed him by the arms and led him out. As he went through the crowd, several people spit on him. A few women smacked him. However, his body was so numb that Timothy couldn't feel a thing.

Chapter 45

SEVEN YEARS LATER...

It had been nearly a decade since Sherie and Denise met one another. Even though it was against client-counselor policy, they still managed to become excellent friends. There wasn't a day that went by in which they didn't band together.

Now, out of the blue, they built up enough courage to visit the Tennessee State Prison. They pulled up around 9:30 a.m. in Denise's blue Hyundai. They got out of the vehicle together and checked in to be approved. A half hour later, they finally made it past the long line of visitors and were called in opposite directions. Sherie was directed down the west wing to visit her dad, and Denise was called to the east wing. Neither of them had been to a prison before, so they were nervous and had no clue what they were going to say to the people they came to see.

Denise was in the isolation section for fifteen more minutes before the man was escorted out by two officers. The man looked up at her, then her child that she had brought along. They stared at each other through the glass before either of them picked the phone's receiver up.

"Hey..." Timothy said curiously. He was surprised that

anyone came to see him because he had never had a single visit since he'd been incarcerated.

"Hi. How are you? I know you probably don't know who we are, but..."

"I know exactly who you are, and I know the reason you came. I want you to forgive me for the things I have done to you." He cut her off and took over the conversation in his most sincere voice. "I found Christ since I've been on death row, and I've had a change of heart. I have repented over and over again. If I have been cursed and condemned on earth, then at least I can be reconciled in heaven."

"Uh. I'm glad you found Christ and all, but I'm not here to be concerned about your life," she said. "I brought my daughter here so she can see her father. She has wondered who her father was for the last past seven years. She says all the kids at school have a daddy except for her."

Timothy was shocked. After all this time that had passed by, he never imagined that he had impregnated one of the victims. And for her to not have an abortion showed that she was a good woman that loved life. Tears welled up in his eyes then began to roll down his cheeks. He was speech-less. This little mixed girl resembled him.

"Come here, Cara!" Denise yelled out to the child who was in the corner playing with her imaginary friend. "Here is your daddy."

The little girl didn't hesitate to grab the phone. She was so excited. "Are you my daddy?" She screamed in elation.

He couldn't speak. He barely nodded his head, indicating yes. "Why are you up in here? When you coming home? Are you going to take me to class?" She asked question after question.

Timothy stared at her long, curly hair and yellow

complexion. He saw himself inside his daughter's eyes.

"Why aren't you saying anything? Why are you crying, Daddy?" She patronized him without knowing it. "Mom, I don't think Dad's ready to talk to me right now." She said it so innocently. "I will talk to him later." She handed her mom back the phone then observed her father's actions.

Denise held the phone in her hand and thought to herself for a moment. This was a terrible situation for herself and her daughter. One day she was going to have to tell little Cara the truth of how she was conceived, but for now she would give her bits and pieces of the revelation. Denise hung up the phone without looking Timothy in the face. She motioned for her daughter to leave with her. They left out the door while Denise fought back her emotions.

When the guards saw that inmate Douglas' visit was over, they went over to him and wrestled to get him out of the seat because he put up a fight. He wasn't ready to release that vapor of his life, so he wanted to sit there as long as possible.

It was hard to resist with all the shackles and chains on, so the guards managed to snatch him up then headed toward the death row quarters. By the time they passed the riot gates and controller's office, a gang of inmates popped up from nowhere. They began to beat the guards with locks and batteries wrapped up in socks. Timothy was looking incredulously and didn't know what to do. He hadn't been around another person in seven years. He ate, slept, watched TV, showered, and used the restroom in his solitary cell. After the group of Mexicans beat the officers into comas, two of them stabbed Timothy Douglas to death. This is why people should be careful who they harm because they can end up in prison with the victims' family members.

Chapter 46

I t was 4:42 a.m. on a rainy night. The weather was cold and quiet as Captain Smith laid asleep in his studio apartment. His phone had been ringing since 3:00 in the morning, but he decided to ignore it, but it wouldn't stop vibrating. "Hello?!" he answered in a gritty voice.

"Hey!" the woman on the other end of the line cried out. She sounded like she'd been crying for days, and he imagined puffs under her eyes and around her nose. "I hate myself for divorcing you. I haven't been able to sleep in months. I made the worst decision of my life letting you go. I am so sorry. Please come home to me. I miss you so much. I will do whatever it takes to make up with you." Snot was dripping from her nose as she pleaded her case. "I love you so much. I really do." She put the phone to the side for a minute to blow the green boogers out her nose.

Smith heard everything that was going on in the background. He wouldn't dare allow himself to go through the turmoil that his ex-wife put him through again. He put the phone down on the dresser then pressed the "end talk" button. To hang up on her was just a minor symbol of what he really wanted to do. He wiggled his body into the mattress to regain his comfort. He then whispered to himself, "I must remember to get my number changed in the morning."

A Letter to My Readers

Dear Readers,

I am an innocent man who has been wrongly convicted of a murder that occurred on Halloween night in 2007 on Stanton Road in Little Rock, Arkansas. If you can assist in any way with the help of my appeals, or if you have any information regarding the incident or the actual perpetrators involved, please contact me via the information provided below. Anything will be helpful and remain confidential at your request. My family has prepared a reward for those who come forth with helpful information.

With sincerest gratitude,
Rahsaan Taylor
Justice For Rahsaan
c/o Rahsaan Taylor
P.O. Box 193302
Little Rock, AR 72219
alphaomegamk2@gmail.com
(501) 541-9279

Contact the Author

Send all fanmail, pictures, and ideas, or comments to:
Rahsaan Taylor ADC#147955
P.O. Box 500
Grady, AR 71644

I would love to hear from you! Your decisions, thoughts, and comments are very valuable to me. Maybe we can get together and write a book or maybe your recommendations can inspire me to write another book of any kind.

-Rahsaan

Acknowledgments

In all of my books that I have written, I always give full recognition to Yahweh, who is the center and head of my life. Yahweh, I have been through a lot and suffered many times. I am human, so, at times, my faith has wavered, but, through it all, I know that somewhere and somehow there is a God. I may not understand all things, so I solely depend upon you. I love you, Lord, my King. I pray that I may be blessed beyond measure along with my family, loved ones, fans and friends. Amen.

To my grandmother, who is also the mother of her church, you have set a great example of how your seeds and your seed's seeds should walk.

To my granddad ("Pee-Wee"), I love you, man, and I will never forget all those bikes you brought for us back in the early nineties. You have always done good deeds and protected us.

To my dad (Samuel Taylor), somehow I failed to mention your name in my other books. Oh, how one must forgive to be free. I am so much like you. However, once the mud is cleared, I discover which attributes to keep and which ones to throw away. I love you with the love of a son. Furthermore, I love you with the Love of God. You are my role model and hero.

To my mother, I could be in the midst of a storm, and

just the thought of you would make me calm. I remember when I was young and would get into it with a girlfriend or regular friend. They would say that they were about to call the police, teacher, or someone else who they
figured I would fear. However, I never paid them attention unless they tried to call Momma. Only then would I cooperate. They never knew, but to me, fear actually means to love and respect. With that being said, know that you will always be honored.

Special thanks to Coral Smith and Ray Jones. I appreciate you two for taking care of my sisters and loving them. You have beautiful wives, who are very good women, so don't mess that up. I know that we are all men, but we still have vows. (You know what I'm talking about.) Much love, my brothers!

Blessings to my siblings, Shekila, Keith, Nioka, and Tichina. Thank you all for sticking by my side. Being in the belly of the beast is not easy, but it is less hard when I can develop strength from the four of you.

To my wonderful children, Mariyah and Zi'Yaan. I miss you so much. By chance, we were set apart, but by destiny we will unite. May God protect you from all evil and cover you from corruption. Continue to strive for perfection and never get involved in the wrong crowd. Choose your friends wisely and always make the right decisions.

Next, I want to give a shout-out to all the people who are locked behind those bars or once were. Some make mistakes and do better because they are forgiven, while others' mistakes by no means can be repaired or made up for.

Wherever you are, you can make a difference, whether it is mediocre or major. I am one who believes that God can make a way where there is no way. We may be afflicted in order to teach others to follow the correct path.

The following are names of people I have been incarcerated alongside. Most of you kept it solid with me; some of you were partially real, but I added your name in my book because you assisted me in same form or fashion in the way that I needed it. Even if you aren't one thousand, I still have to be. To others, this is an apology for me overthinking a situation.

Remember that even if our bodies are locked up, our spirits, minds, and social skills can still be free. We will one day soar beyond expectation.

I am much obliged to: Mr. Mayne Dank, Grayson, Milwaukee, Rey, Bam, T.J., Art A.K.A. JD, Saddiq, Wolfe, Harvey Bond, Yount, Jacobi, Buck, Mel-Wayne, Mendenhall, Young one, Lil' One, Lil' Ed, Ron Kelley, Alimen, Richard Hill, Theodis Kelley, Roe-Roe, K.G., Ken, Big O, Stuart, Dickerson, Mr. Orr A.K.A. Treat, Hustle, L.A. Rob, Muhummad, Ray D, Big, Ralph Armstrong, K.D., Dexter, Duke, Ju-Box, Big Youngster, Simp, J.V., Psych, O-Dogg, Zoom, Watson-El, Pete, Ohio A.K.A Danny Boy, Tate, Slim, Shaw, Scooby, Khaliq, Lil' E, Robert King Jr., Ronald O'Neal, Mr. Houston, Nick, Pierre, Charlie Brown, Big E, E-Dubb, B-Lo, D-L, Mayne-Mayne, E a.k.a. Eric, B., Mario, Villagram, Snoop, Cap, J-Rock, Smiley, Squirrel, Bryan, Head, Swift, N.O., Carl Lindell, Phillips, Nemi A.K.A Morgan, Gary Parker, Shorty Mac, Roy, G.Q., Westbrook, K-Rock, Charles Rodgers, J-Boog face, E-Lo, Ford, D-3, Joe Moore, Shahid Farrakhan, Mud, Lil Pat, Hammer,

Debo, Fat Boy, Jabry D., Tubbs, Aldridge A.K.A. Double A, Strokes, Razorback, Cody Childress, 9-0, Whitherspoon, Abraham Grant, Red, Johnny Taylor, Cherry, B.J., Terrence Manuel A.K.A. Five Deuce, Big Drew, Duck, P-Nutt, Big Tex, Laswell, Lil' Larry, Tuck, Morehead, Wedgeworth, Lonnie Mitchell, Paray, Big Jeff.

I can't forget the women who keep it real, for the time being. You encouraged me and gave me something to take my mind off my troubles. I have to give a bunch of thanks to: Cassandra, Buffy (a.k.a. Eleasha Brown), Tamara Arthurs, Stephany Miller, Sandra Lewis, Lynette, Victoria Davis, Clara Davis, Carrie, Shay (a.k.a. Reshonda Carter), Sharonda Hegg, Frieda Broadnax, Brenda Pickett, Shaquille Berkeley, Katrina, Allison, Vanessa Ferroa, Clarissa, Angela Whitfield (a.k.a. Peaches), Lisa Jean Cardinal, Patichel Porter, NeNe, Shelia Wilson, Sharonda White, Chanel Roddy, Nicole Swoopes, Paulette Roth, Kate Come, Vickie Shreveport, Evangelist Vera Rivers, and Tamilko.

ABOUT THE AUTHOR

RAHSAAN AKI TAYLOR is a versatile author. He writes urban books, horror stories, theology/spiritual books, anthropology, devotionals, and books based on true life experiences. He graduated college at Lincoln University (formerly NADC), but has advanced with his passion to write. Rahsaan is the father of two wonderful children, Zi'yaan and Mariyah Taylor. He now resides in the INJUSTICE SYSTEM OF ARKANSAS.

J. Kenkade
PUBLISHING®

Our Motto
"Transforming Life Stories"

Also Available from
THE AUTHOR

ISBN: 978-1-944486-04-4
Purchase at www.jkenkadepublishing.com

Each day, we are faced with challenges that we must conquer and overcome. The contents of this book will help you maintain, stay afloat, and solve some of your troubles. There is a skill, a strategy, and an art to living a prosperous and peaceful life

Also Available from
THE AUTHOR

ISBN: 978-1-944486-12-9
Purchase at www.jkenkadepublishing.com

We all have wondered why bad things happen to us or someone we love. Often times, we never receive the answer to the questions that are asked. Therefore, the content of this book enlightens you on many topics and situations. It will reveal the hidden things of God. Discover insights on: Increasing your faith; Prophecies; The characteristics of thinking and ability of men and women; Prayers; Is religion acceptable or not? The symbolical meaning of numbers; Relationships, and much more!

Also Available from
J. Kenkade Publishing

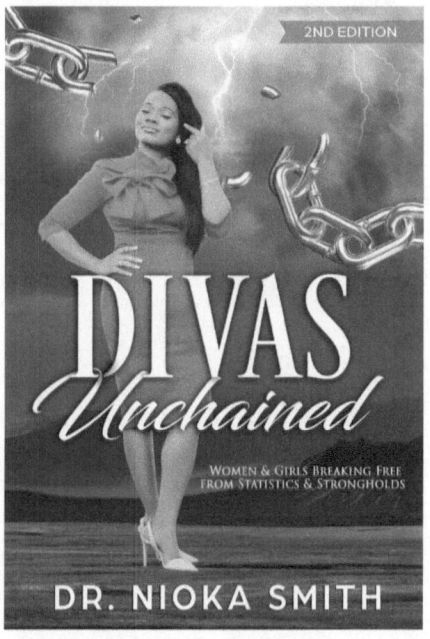

ISBN: 978-1-944486-25-9
Purchase at www.drniokasmith.com

DIVAS Unchained is the powerful chain-breaking reality of the many unfortunate strongholds our women and girls face and of one woman whose painful past almost killed her, until the voice of the Lord guided her into reversing Satan's plan. Dr. Nioka uses her divine gift to help women and girls break free from destructive life cycles and prosper in all areas of life. Discover what has been holding you back and take a journey as you see yourself within each turning page. Satan has lied to you. It's time to expose his lies. It's time to break free!

Also Available from
J. Kenkade Publishing

ISBN: 978-1-944486-42-6
Purchase at www.jkenkadepublishing.com

A major stroke interrupted her life at the tender age of 19, when life was just beginning for her. Find out how this stroke survivor fought against the attack on her own brain to defeat the odds within her physical, spiritual, emotional, and even her academic life.

www.ingramcontent.com/pod-product-compliance
Lightning Source LLC
Chambersburg PA
CBHW050401260626
47156CB00003B/822